ELLIE'S DREAM

Elaheh Mortazavi

Independently Published

CONTENTS

CHAPTER ONE

At the age of nine, Ellie was a lonely girl who didn't have any friends and only found safety and peace with horses while being around them and spending time with them. Every weekend, Ellie and her Mum would go to Hyde park to watch the horses and ponies. She would stroke, cuddle, and kiss them if she had the chance. As she spent more time with horses, she felt they were the most reliable and loyal friends she had. This fact and these feelings made her fall in love with them. Ellie felt she could be her real self when she was around them and wasn't afraid of making mistakes or them laughing at her because of her appearance. As this bond deepened, she felt such an intense passion for horses which made her wish to become a professional horse-rider in the future.

Ellie was a girl of average height with a slender physique and a round face. Her mother had passed her genes to her and was an average height with curly auburn-coloured hair as well. Ellie resembled a younger version of her mother. She always wore her round glasses with a green-coloured frame. She was called 'Four-eyes' by some of her mean classmates. Or even 'Carrot Top' because of her red hair. Those nasty kids loved to bully and insult her whenever given the opportunity. She hated school in total. She thought life would have been much easier and more pleasant without schools to attend. In Ellie's opinion, schools were horrible places, which just made one depressed and nervous. And of course, somewhere to be constantly bullied by other children. To her, school meant a place for torture.

Ellie was a very sensitive and vulnerable girl. Ellie had low self-confidence and never really believed in herself or her talents. Also, she didn't have patience in seeing results and whenever she didn't get good outcomes immediately, she would give up on that thing and say she's not meant for doing it or she wasn't talented enough.

The bullying at school had really taken the toll on her and influenced her in every possible way. She preferred to stay in her room while at home.

Charlotte, her best and only friend, had shoulder length, straight, shiny dark-brown hair and hazel-coloured eyes. She was raised in a caring family. Her parents, Mr and Mrs Melton, were both teachers at the primary school. Their houses were rather close, only a few blocks away from each other in the same neighbourhood. Charlotte's family lived in Manchester two years ago, before moving into their current home.

Ellie knew Charlotte back from when she was seven.

◆ ◆ ◆

Monday came, which meant waking up early and going to school until the next weekend, which seemed an eternity away. Ellie hated Mondays. She stretched her hand and switched on the little oval porcelain bed lamp which stood on her bedside table. She watched the clock on the wall. It struck seven forty. Today she'd woken up earlier than usual. She tried to sleep again and pulled her floral pink and white cotton duvet up to her nose, making herself warm and cosy.

After a few minutes of struggling to fall back to sleep, Ellie decided it's useless, and she'd better get up. As frustrated as she was, she lazily got out of her bed and stood in front of her small round wooden mirror hanging on the patterned cream wallpaper. She picked up her comb from the bedside drawer and dragged it through her curly, frizzy, red hair. She winced as she detangled her hair and the tangles pulled. "OUCH!" She only detangled half of her hair, and that was enough to satisfy her. She didn't really bother about it to be too neatly combed and she didn't make a fuss about her overall appearance in general, anyway. She normally looked scruffy when she woke up early in the morning to go to school. At that time of the day, she was usually too tired to bother with her style. So, she just pulled her hair back and tied it with a loose elastic hair band, as she would normally do.

She opened her dark wooden dresser and picked up her school uniform, which was tossed there in an unorderly way. The uniform was a grey skirt, white buttoned shirt, and a navy cardigan. Ellie reluctantly put them on and gently tiptoed on the creaky floorboards and headed downstairs, trying her best not to make too much noise.

While going downstairs, her eye fell on her Mum who was still asleep in her room next to the living room, her snores drifting from her bedroom. Quietly, so not to wake her up, Ellie went to the bathroom and washed her face with lukewarm water and headed to the kitchen. She started getting the breakfast ready. She opened the cupboard, searching for some biscuits. She found some which were dried out from being kept in the cupboard for too long. She made a facial gesture being frustrated; she left them there, closed the cupboard, and instead had some hot tea with toast. She set the kettle to boil for tea, dropped a tea bag into the teapot, buttered her toast, and began chewing on it while she poured some tea for herself in a porcelain cup. She tucked her hair behind her ears, took a bite of her toast and watched the raindrops running down the windowpane. "I'm going to be drenched before I even get halfway to school," Ellie muttered as she took another sip of her tea. She finished her breakfast and got up from the plastic chair and went to the door. Quickly slipping on her black rubber wellington boots, she headed for school. She closed the door quietly despite her habit of slamming the door shut, so she wouldn't wake her Mum up with the sound of it.

They lived on 45 Saint Patrick's street, in a narrow old dingy house built of rusty red bricks. The front gate looked old and creaked loudly as it opened. As Ellie stepped outside, the wind, which gusted around the house, blew the rain into her face. She ducked her head into her raincoat and went to fetch her bike from the shed. She climbed on to her bike and pedalled up the steep hill towards school. Rainy days were the worst, especially while pedalling, since it made her glasses steam up and limited her vision.

She had pedalled less than halfway to school. As Ellie wheeled to the side of the road, a careless driver in a huge van steered exactly into the big puddle on the road beside Ellie and splashed a great amount of muddy water on her. Ellie stopped instantly and stared at the van with a serious look in her eyes. She blinked in disbelief and yelled, "Look at what you've done to me!" She rolled her eyes in frustration. But it was too late, and the driver was already out of sight, leaving Ellie wet and stained with mud. Her glasses were sprayed with water, which blurred her eyesight. She took off her round, green-rimmed glasses and wiped them clean with her scarf. She mounted her bike and continued her way, pedalling as fast as she could.

Finally, after a good twenty minutes of pedalling up the hill, Ellie arrived at school exhausted and soaking wet under the heavy rain. As soon as she entered the building, Ellie tore off her wet and dirty coat and hung it over on the classroom peg next to the radiator to dry out. By the time she sat behind her desk, she was feeling very cold and was shivering. Hopefully, Charlotte came to support her and lent Ellie her extra warm jacket to wear while her raincoat was drying out.

They had art during the first hour and pupils were to sit and work in pairs. They had to paint their face masks, which they made for a school play they were going to demonstrate the next week. Their art teacher, Mrs Bell, went out of the classroom to print some papers for the class while children were busy with their artwork.

Ellie stood up and walked past Jane's desk to sharpen her coloured pencils in the rubbish bin, which was put in front of the class, when suddenly her foot caught on the carpet. She lost her footing and stumbled. As she was falling, her elbow accidentally hit a bottle of red paint and knocked it over on to Jane's desk and the paint splashed on Jane's jumper and uniform. Ellie didn't mean to make things go wrong, but somehow, she always made terrible mistakes.

"Oh. My. Gosh! What do you think you're playing at?" Jane was shocked. Then she pulled her jumper in front of her and said with bitterness, "Look what you've done to my jumper. You ruined it!" She leapt up from her table with a tense expression. Her face had become bright red.

"Seriously, why can you never manage to do things

without making a mess, Ellie?" Jane raised her voice. "Besides, you don't even have the money to buy me a new one because you are poor and your Mum cannot pay for it. Seriously, you're good for nothing, Ellie. Shame on you!" The entire class had become quiet and everyone was looking at Jane and Ellie, who stood in the middle of the room. There were sounds of whispering across the class.

"I… I'm so sorry Jane. I didn't mean to. I… I… accidentally tripped over and fell," said Ellie. She had a sudden feeling as if her bloodstream was flowing into her throat, blocking the airways and making her unable to speak properly. Her voice was shaking. Ellie had become red and hot in the face and acted flustered, pressing her fingers hard together. Whenever Ellie felt nervous or stressed, her eyes twitched badly, causing her eyes to blink excessively.

"For heaven's sake, you have four eyes. How could you just not see in front of you?" said Jane, as she pointed towards Ellie's glasses. At that moment, Ellie was totally speechless and wished she hadn't come to school in the first place.

Then, to make the matters worse, Jane faced Ellie and folded her arms. She added, "By the way, I must add: of course, you cannot become a horse-rider, Ellie. Horses are for rich people, not poor lousy people like you." Ellie's heart shattered in pieces when she heard her say those mean words. The words felt like a venomous snake biting her and injecting poison into her heart and soul. Ellie just remained there, unable to move and was staring blankly at her. She didn't even have the energy to answer back. Her best friend Charlotte came to her aid.

"Mind your mouth, Jane! How dare you be so rude to my friend. You are so nasty!" replied Charlotte with a tense tone and hands on her hips. At least she had the nerves to stand up to Jane, unlike Ellie.

"*Oh*, look who has come to speak up and take her side defending her? Has cat bit your tongue, Ellie?" said Jane, with a sense of sarcasm in her voice. "Maybe she doesn't have a tongue herself?" She giggled with her friends, who were sitting around the table next to her.

Ellie felt a lump forming in her throat. She was so embarrassed in front of other classmates and was in tears by then. She was grateful their teacher wasn't in the classroom. At that moment, the door opened and Mrs Bell came in. The whole class fell silent and Jane sat down at her table, flashing Ellie a piercing look. Ellie and Charlotte went to their desks and sat down. "Are you okay Ellie?" whispered Charlotte, who was sitting next to Ellie.

"Yeah, I'm fine, thanks", replied Ellie with a low voice and put on a brave smile. Charlotte smiled in sympathy and put her hands on Ellie's lap. Ellie wanted to hold on to the comforting feeling of her only friend for as long as she could. Since Ellie was a shy girl and an introvert, she hardly made any friends and she was lucky to have found Charlotte as her close friend, who she could rely on anytime.

Jane was their mean and selfish classmate who usually caused Ellie trouble. Jane had green eyes and long, straight, shiny blonde hair, which almost stood down on her waist and had a pointed nose. She was tall with long slim legs which looked like they belonged to a model. The top of Ellie's head reached up to Jane's shoulders, which made Ellie feel self-conscious about her own height when she was standing next to her. Ellie couldn't help but feel jealous of her height and her immaculate appearance. She was one of those girls who cared a lot about her looks, acting like a grown-up lady. Her nails were neatly manicured and her hair looked so stunning, as if she'd been to a beauty salon before school.

Jane's parents were rich and had spoiled her rotten. She lived like a princess at home, always having whatever she wished. Her parents both worked in a private company as the Head managers. They never spent enough quality time raising their daughter and didn't bother teaching her good manners. All they cared about was *money*. They had a huge, elegant, two-storey house with a magnificent swimming pool in front of it. Jane had whatever a girl at her age could dream of, from barbie dolls, many games and toys, to a tree house and separate dance and ballet room for herself. She was raised by a nanny for most of her life and hadn't seen her parents as much.

She was a self-centred girl who didn't care for anyone except herself. From what Ellie had heard from other kids, Jane's Mum seems very easy-going and carefree who lets Jane do anything she wants. She buys Jane new clothes and stuff every week. She even lets Jane wear lip gloss to school or do makeup and wear mascara on the weekends. Jane and her Mum spent most of their time together in high-end shops or in beauty salons styling their hair, manicuring, or pedicuring.

However, there was this good quality about Jane: she cared a lot about the environment and animals. She loved growing green plants, watering and nurturing them carefully. This was something she was fond of. She had also joined the "Green Planet" group at school where, as group members, they take care of trees and plants and all greeneries and environment at school. Recently, Jane had decided she wanted to be a *vegetarian*. She had said it's horrible and selfish of us human beings to kill poor animals and eat their meat.

As soon as school finished and the bell rang for going home, Ellie rushed out of the classroom and marched into the corridors. Outside, the heavy rain had given way to a fine drizzle and Ellie decided it was dry enough to cycle home. Ellie's bike was an old rusty bike which had belonged to her Mum during her childhood years. She had leaned it against a tree outside the schoolyard and locked it with a chain. It was wet on the surface, so she patted the saddle dry with her sleeves and mounted her bike, placing her schoolbag in the front basket. The path was so slippery that Ellie had to steer her bike on the road carefully. She tried to pedal as fast as the wet path allowed her to and went towards home as quickly as possible. She gripped the handlebars tighter and clenched her toes to keep the large wellies on her feet. As Ellie blinked, the tears in her eyes ran down her cheeks and from time to time, Ellie wiped them off with the back of her hand.

When Ellie got home, she was too upset to even ring the doorbell and wait for her Mum to open it. She gently turned the key inside the keyhole and entered the house. She found her Mum sitting in the corner of the living room, busy sewing a dress for one of her customers. Mum was quite startled to see Ellie inside the house. "Good heavens! When did you come in Ellie? You scared me!" said Mum as she stood up.

"Hello, Mum… sorry if I scared you, I didn't mean to. I came in with my key and didn't want to bother with ringing the bell." Ellie went upstairs to her room to hide her sad face from her Mum and change her school clothes. Her room was a low-ceilinged room on the top floor overlooking the main street. The furnishings were cheap, and the wallpaper was peeled off at the corners. Her bed was old, which creaked annoyingly every once in a while.

Ellie put on a casual outdoor outfit. She chose a bright orange woolly jumper, which her Mum had knitted for her and a woolly hat to keep her head warm. The red hat matched the tone of her red hair perfectly. Ellie loved striped socks and had a collection of them in all different colours. She pulled the drawer of her dresser and randomly picked up a pair of stripy socks and put them on, pulling them up to her knees.

She went to Charlotte's to ask if she was up for going to the park together. She always felt better when she saw Charlotte. There was a park not very far from them which was famous for its flower gardens and different flowers planted in them. It also had a not-so-huge greenhouse in the middle of it, which amused people. The park was usually very busy and crowded on weekends, with many visitors. Ellie and Charlotte used to play in its playground, which has an enormous slide, swings, monkey bars, sew-saws, and merry-go-round.

Ellie arrived at the front door of Charlotte's with her rusty old bike and climbed down from it, letting the bike fall on the grass. She looked at their home, thinking what a blessing to have such a friend. The curtains were open, revealing inside the house. She caught sight of Charlotte's Mum in the kitchen. In the hall, Charlotte's youngest sister, who was four years old, was watching cartoons sitting in front of the TV on a velvety blue blanket. Her name was Clara, and she looked totally different from Charlotte, as if she came from another family. She had big blue eyes and bright yellow hair. Charlotte had an older brother too, who was two years older than her. He was sitting on the couch playing with his X-box as usual. His name was Charles and looked quite like Charlotte. Ellie could hear their loud voices coming from inside.

Ellie neared the door and stepped on the doormat. She pressed her index finger on the bell, which was a small button stuck to the wall on the right of their green door. She rang twice just in case she wasn't heard in their busy house. After a few seconds of waiting, Charlotte herself came to the door and opened it. "Hey Ellie, I'm glad to see you again! What's up?"

"Hey Charlotte! Thanks, Me too! Are you up for cycling with our bikes?"

"I would love to. Let me ask my Mum first." Charlotte disappeared into the house, leaving the door half open. She went into the kitchen asking for her Mum's permission.

After a few minutes, she appeared at the door again. "Mum said it's okay; I can go if I won't stay longer than two hours. Let's go then, Ellie!" She smiled from ear to ear with her teeth showing and her hazel-coloured eyes shining in delight under the bright sky. Charlotte, unlike Ellie, was very good looking and even the least beautiful outfits still looked gorgeous on her, which made Ellie feel envious of her. Charlotte's shoulder length dark brown hair matched with a bright pink jacket looked even more stunning. She had put on a pair of white trainers with a navy warm sports trouser. Charlotte picked up her bike, which was laying under the shed. She had a dark pink bike with flowers dangling off the handlebars. Charlotte was very feminine and girlish. Both girls climbed onto their bikes and off they went toward the park. They pedalled side by side and chatted happily all the way there. Ellie loved the humorous side of Charlotte's personality, which made her laugh easily and forget about bad days or bad events in an instant.

CHAPTER TWO

The following day, Ellie woke up with the sound of her alarm clock going off. Along with a big yawn and a full body stretch, she dragged herself out of bed. Ellie was trying her best to become her best version in appearance to impress Jane and her classmates.

She put on her best efforts to brush her shoulder-length, frizzy hair. It was a struggle with so many tangles! She pulled her hair back and tied it in a ponytail. Ellie wished she had straight hair, just like many other girls who she knew. She noticed her glasses were dirty, with fingerprints all over the glass. She took them under the sink in the bathroom and turned on the tap water and washed the glasses using some hand washing liquid. Then she put on some strawberry flavoured lip balm to glaze her thin lips, making them appear fuller and plumped. She pinched her cheeks to give them a natural blush, just in the same way as she had seen her Mum do.

When she went to put on her black wellington boots, she wiped them with a cloth to clean off the dirt, making them shine. Ellie seemed pleased with her look. She looked at herself one more time in the tall mirror hanging on the wall next to the entrance door before heading to school.

They had maths in the first hour. Pupils were all quietly seated in their chairs, staring at their maths teacher in silence. "Ellie Patterson," Mrs Rudolf called out her name as she handed each pupil their exam results. She walked along the class and handed their papers with their marks on them. She got close to Ellie's desk. Ellie's stomach was in knots as she waited. Mrs Rudolf looked at Ellie as she gave her exam result to her. She nodded her head as a sign of expressing her pity for Ellie, "Another C minus." Ellie's stomach lurched, and she felt miserable for always getting the worst marks in the class. She hated herself for that.

A few of her classmates laughed and whispered nasty things to her. "*Ewww*, Ellie is always the lazy one. She cannot get any marks higher than C," said Jane as she giggled. "Look at my A+," she said proudly, showing off her high grades to Ellie. "Maybe it has something to do with your redhead and your poor eye vision?" Then she laughed even louder, making Ellie's eyes fill with tears and her face turn hot from shame.

What's wrong with me? Maybe my IQ is the lowest among the others? Maybe I should attend the school for children with lower IQs? Ellie felt sick by the thoughts and the questions dancing in her head. She flinched and squeezed her toes under the table.

"*Sshhh*! Quiet please, I don't want to hear nonsense," Mrs Rudolf hit hard on her table and pointed her index finger towards Jane and pursed her lips, looking furious.

That night Ellie cried herself to sleep with her pillows wet with tears from what Jane had said to her in the classroom that day in front of the other classmates. She felt like a loser.

Jane always made fun of Ellie and tried to ruin her self-image by constantly telling her she wouldn't be able to succeed in anything and cannot get what she wants because she can't do things right and calling her "Lame" or "Bumbler" or "Good-for-nothing."

Jane had once passed Ellie a note under the table in the classroom in which she had written such a nasty thing to Ellie: YOU CAN NEVER REACH YOUR GOALS BECAUSE YOU ARE SO CLUMSY AND DUMB! These words made Ellie question her abilities and crippled her with self-doubt.

◆ ◆ ◆

At the weekend, Ellie's Grandma came to their house to visit her daughter and granddaughter. Ellie's Grandparents were in their late sixties and lived in the suburbs of London. They preferred to live in a quiet place far from the busy city streets, traffic, and pollution. On weekends, usually Mum and Ellie paid visits to Ellie's grandparents, but this time instead her grandma visited them. That day in the morning they all went out for a walk and then to their local Theatre to watch a Mary Poppins play, which Ellie really loved. After they got back home, they all longed for a nice hot tea to wash away their late afternoon drowsiness.

Grandma was sitting on the rocking chair in the living room, gently sipping from her tea with her shaky hands and commenting on the bad weather and talking about her daily life and grown-up stuff, which made Ellie bored. As Ellie was sitting on a chair, busy swinging her feet, suddenly her foot hit the coffee table in front of her, tipping her teacup, causing all the hot liquid to splash on the beige carpet.

"What are you doing Ellie?" her Mum cried as she jumped out of her chair to bring the mop and some liquid to wash the stained carpet.

Ellie was embarrassed and didn't want this to happen. "I'm so sorry, Mum." Her cheeks flushed, turning to beetroot. She went to the bathroom next to the living room to splash some cold water on her face.

When Grandma made sure that she and Ellie's Mum were alone, she leaned over to Ellie's Mum and cleared her throat. "Ellie is becoming a big girl now and she'll soon turn Ten. She should stop being clumsy and acting poorly. I think she should learn to believe in herself and have a higher self-confidence. No wonder she keeps failing at things and is bullied by other children her age at school."

Ellie was eavesdropping as she was standing in the bathroom and could hear what her Grandma said about her. Unable to bear it, Ellie stamped her foot on the wooden ground so hard that made dust fly into the air. She felt miserable at hearing such words, and she huffed and puffed her way up the stairs to her room. She was mad at her grandma for saying such a nasty thing about her, and she clenched her hands into a fist. She was so cross she stayed in her room for most of the day and didn't come down except for lunch.

Before lunch, Ellie went out to breathe some fresh air, hoping it would change her mood. She wanted to get as far as possible from the atmosphere in the house. "Don't be back late. We'll be having lunch in an hour, Ellie," Mum called after her.

"I won't be long", said Ellie without looking. She fetched her rusty bike from the shed. The weather was crisp and cold, clouds were gathering overhead. She paused and breathed in the fresh air, listening to the rustling of the tall, wild green grass and the bushes surrounding their house. She hoisted her bike onto the pavement, hopped on it, and pedalled freely, releasing her negative feelings. As she sped up on the asphalt on the road, she loosened the grip of her left hand from the handlebar and put it high in the air, waving. Her loose red hair was flying backwards in the wind. She went to the woods, which was not far from their house, only twenty minutes of cycling. Ellie loved the feeling of freedom she had over there in the woods, especially when she passed across the tall trees overshadowing the path with their flat, broad leaves. The cool breeze on her face felt good and blew away her grumpiness.

She returned home in time as she'd promised her Mum. As she walked into the kitchen, she saw the table was already prepared and laid for lunch. They had chicken breast with steamed broccoli and carrots, along with freshly squeezed orange juice. Ellie took a seat while hanging her napkin around her neck and poured some orange juice into her glass. As her grandma walked through the kitchen, humming and singing, Ellie played with her fork and spoon to avoid looking at her. Ellie didn't want to look into her grandma's eyes after what she had heard earlier. However, Ellie tried to pretend she hadn't heard them talking behind her back and acted indifferently. But her grandma was too polite and adoring, so Ellie couldn't let her down or avoid her eyes. She then decided not to bear a grudge against her grandma anymore and instead forgive her in her heart. Ellie then smiled at her grandma as she put food on Ellie's plate.

The next day, on Sunday morning, Ellie and her Mum went to Hyde park in central London to see the ponies there, as they usually did on weekends. This had become a routine of theirs for over a year. The sun was setting behind the trees, and her Mum had already grown tired of being out in that big park standing on her feet for hours. She had only managed to get a little sleep the night before and meanwhile, she also had a lot of work waiting to be done at home; finishing sewing a customer's evening frock, tidying up the house, vacuuming the floors and dusting the shelf tops and surfaces.

Their bus journey back home took them nearly two hours and by the time they got home, they were too exhausted to do anything. Ellie wished they had the money to buy a car and lead a more peaceful life like her classmates, instead of taking the bus. Ellie took a weary breath and yawned. They just lay on the couch and watched television.

"How about I go and make some hot chocolate for us and you bring some of those biscuits in the tin to eat with?" Mum suggested. Their body craved the sugar to boost their energy.

"That sounds great to me!" agreed Ellie.

Ellie sat in front of the television holding the TV controller in her hand, switching between channels, until she found a show that she considered *entertaining*. It was a documentary about wild horses running freely in their natural habitat. Her eyes were glued to the programme.

Ellie was obsessed with horses and had posters of them on the walls of her room. She believed horses were majestic creatures. She had always longed to have a horse or pony herself and become a professional horse-rider one day and join the show-jumping competitions and even win a medal. It was her greatest passion since she was three years old. Unlike other girls the same age as her who were in love with dolls, Ellie had been fascinated with ponies. Therefore, on her birthdays or at Christmas, she had usually been given different toy horses or things related to horses as presents. And Ellie was thrilled by them. She even owned a few books about horses and horse-riding sports such as show-jumping. For Ellie, horses were the cutest, most adorable animals on earth. She was curious to discover and understand all about their world. But unfortunately, her family neither had the money to afford the horse-riding training fees, nor could afford to buy or lease the horse itself.

After the programme was finished, Ellie went upstairs and spread all her painting stuff and brushes on her desk and sat down to paint a picture. A beautiful huge house with lovely green scenery in the background. She loved to paint pictures of her wishes and kept them in a folder. It made her feel amazing, as if the paintings were real.

CHAPTER THREE

One snowy Saturday morning in February, Ellie woke up happy and euphoric about the dream she had. She pulled the curtain away and looked out the window. Snow was falling and landing softly on the ground, which had created a spectacular landscape. The sky had a fascinating violet tone in it and was clear and bright. The leaves on the trees and the cars parked in the street were all covered with a thin layer of dazzling white snow. Ellie could hear the birds singing their early morning songs.

If not for her dream, Ellie would have had otherwise preferred to sleep in till noon. She wasn't an early bird by nature and loved to sleep in on weekends. Her Mum called her *'night owl'*, since she loved staying up till late, remaining awake past her required bedtime.

Without a doubt, Ellie became determined more than ever to do something and act on it to live her dream life and fulfil her passion. She jumped out of bed with such great excitement. She didn't even bother to make her bed or comb her hair. She pumped her fist in the air and roared with joy, "Hip hip hurray!"

Ellie put on her slippers and hurried down the worn wooden staircase by taking a few steps at a time, singing to herself and dancing all the way to the kitchen to find her Mum. She followed the lovely smells of freshly baked gingerbread and she appeared in the kitchen doorway in her striped dressing gown. She found her Mum in the kitchen in her apron, standing behind the breakfast table, busy preparing them breakfast. Mum had made three pancakes each and served them in separate dishes.

"Morning, Mum," said Ellie as she went into the kitchen.

Her Mum was surprised to see her early in the morning as it wasn't like her to be up at that time. "Oh Ellie, good morning, dear. What made you get up this early on a Saturday morning?" her Mum asked, eyeing her curiously.

Mum went to the fridge and glanced around inside it, looking for the bottle of milkshake. "We seem to have run out of milkshakes… we have to buy them today at the supermarket," she said as she handed Ellie a piece of her hot, freshly baked gingerbread. "You look like you are excited about something, huh?"

Ellie took a chair, sat on it, grabbed her glass of milk in her hand from the table and took a big gulp of it. She wiped her milk-stained mouth and said with bright sparkling eyes, "guess what, Mum?"

She was beaming at her mother with milk being trapped at the corners of her mouth. Her curly red hair was a tangled mess of curls from when she woke up. The scene made her Mum smile. Ellie took a first satisfying bite from the gingerbread, munching noisily. "Mmm… it tastes wonderful. I love the spicy smell of it." As she was chewing on it, Ellie was daydreaming about what she had in her mind. Her large blue eyes grew wider with amusement and didn't even hear her Mum talking to her.

"Ellie? I was actually talking to you." Mum disturbed her thoughts, which startled Ellie, dragging her back to reality.

She noticed her mother's voice and snapped out of her daydream. "Err, sorry Mum, I didn't hear you," she said in a low voice, picking her hair out of her eyes. "I had a wonderful dream last night in which I was an equestrian competing at a show jumping competition, placing a second winning a silver medal! Wow, I even owned a horse which was a brown-coloured one, one of those which I always loved! And I felt like the happiest girl on Earth standing there among the crowd and they were all applauding and shouting my name. Can you imagine that, Mum? I wish I can make my dream come true."

"Yes, yes, my lovely girl. That was an amazing dream." Mum looked into Ellie's sky-blue eyes and couldn't resist giving her a big hug and then stroked her bright red hair. Mum shyly added, "but sadly, I don't think it's possible to pursue your dream since it's too expensive, and as you know dear, I don't earn that much money by sewing." Her Mum was embarrassed to say so and to let her daughter down.

"Yeah, I know Mum, I understand and I don't want to put pressure on you," Ellie said sympathetically as the corner of her lips were pulled down.

"Maybe we'll see what we can do about it later, okay?" She patted on Ellie's back, giving her some hope. She faced Ellie and touched her cheeks. "There is nothing wrong with having big dreams. You're a young girl and surely you will find a way to it." They continued chatting over breakfast, and later each went to their respective rooms, starting their daily routines.

Ellie went to her bedroom upstairs and silently closed the door behind her. Her lips were quivering. Ellie sat on her bed and buried her face in her hands. Her eyes filled with tears and a single drop ran down her cheeks. She then started sobbing quietly, to avoid being heard by her Mum.

She thought that life wasn't fair to her. She asked God with frustration, "how can my friends always have what they wish for without worrying about the expenses. Maybe I deserve less than them?" The questions crossed her mind one after the other. Then she stepped near her father's photo, which was sitting on the table beside her bed, and took it in her hands, taking a long look at it for a few minutes. It was a picture of the three of them smiling peacefully when Ellie was at four, while being on a picnic on a sunny day just two weeks before her father's painful death. She gasped sorrowfully.

Ellie had lost her father too soon in a tragic accident on a slippery road on a dark rainy night, five years ago. He had been on his way from Newcastle to London, driving his car when the unfortunate accident occurred. That's mainly the reason which her Mum is overprotective of Ellie. She feared losing her only child and her sole memory of her husband. He was a very kind, generous man and loved helping others. Ellie's dad had worked as a carpenter for most of his life and earned just enough money to make a living and buy them a small house to live in. But overall, they lived with only a little income and were a low-classed family. They'd been in their house for nearly ten years.

Ellie was nine now, an only child who lived with her mother, Mrs Peterson, in London. She remembered little about her father and didn't have vivid memories of him. She was sure she had the best father in the world and he would forever remain a hero to her. Her Mum had given away all her husband's belongings to a shop which collected items for poor people. It was too painful and sad for her to see his clothes or any sort of stuff related to him every day and have them around their home. Mum thought it was easier for her that way to overcome the pain of the loss of her beloved husband. She only kept their photos they had together, which tore her heart to look at, but kept them for the sake of it. She knew Ellie would want to keep the photos of her Dad and look at them to know how her dad looked like. Ellie had the same blue eyes as her father's. Apart from those photos, there was nothing else in the house to remind Ellie of her father. Ellie thought that was a pity since she would have liked to have known more about her father. And his things could have told her a little about him.

Ellie sat down on her bed and pulled her legs up to her body. She was deep in her thoughts when she heard a creak in the floorboards and, in a few seconds, a knock on her door. The door latch was pressed downwards. Her bedroom door flew open; it was her Mum. She gently came in and sat down beside her daughter, wiped Ellie's tears off her face with her hands and tried to calm her. She planted a kiss on Ellie's head. Her heart ached seeing her daughter be so broken-hearted, which brought a painful expression to her face. She promised Ellie she'd do her best to make her biggest dream come true. With that, Ellie cheered up a little and looked at her mother with a smile. She loved her Mum and always took her at her words. They were best friends.

It was afternoon, and Ellie was sitting behind her desk, busy doing her maths homework. She couldn't solve the mathematics problem and was stressed out. She bit on her nails and twirled her hair around her finger as nervous tics when she had to do her maths.

Her Mum brought her a plate which contained sliced fresh fruits for her to eat along with a glass of freshly made orange juice. Ellie wasn't a fan of fruits, but she liked to eat them when her Mum made them into small slices. Mum didn't approve of Ellie eating crisps and all those unhealthy snacks which were nowadays pretty popular among kids, preferring them over healthy food. Her Mum was strict about eating well and avoiding processed foods as much as possible. Especially at Ellie's age, she made sure Ellie received all the necessary vitamins for her growth. Ellie nearly finished the whole plate of fruits only leaving the kiwis, which she didn't feel like eating sour things at that time.

After a while, Ellie was staring out of her window and noticed how quickly the snow was melting on the ground as the sun was gleaming. It had begun to rain, and she could see a huge rainbow formed in the sky. Gradually the rain became heavier and was hitting the glass on the window and the sky darkened to a grey shade. The weather was minus two degrees and freezing. The heater in her room had stopped working, and she was shivering. She saw her breath in the air and her teeth were chattering. She rubbed her hands together quickly and blew heat on them, but her efforts were unsuccessful. So, she got up from her seat, took a blanket, wrapped it around her body and put on her warm striped pink and blue woolly socks to keep herself warm.

When her Mum came up and saw this scene, she scratched her head in a rather annoyed manner. "We should call the repairman to come and fix the radiator again." This was the third time they had to fix it and it would cost them a lot of money. "We should save some money for that," she remarked. "Oh, and we need to first fix the broken washing machine! Good heavens, today that I need it the most, the damned machine has stopped working and now the radiator!" Mum was whining as she bit on her nails.

CHAPTER FOUR

It was Monday, and Ellie always had that Monday morning feeling. She woke up at eight thirty for school, which was quite late. She washed her face, detangled her hair and wore it up in a ponytail. She hurriedly got ready and put on her school uniform. She ate her breakfast cereal, which was her all-time favourite, kissed her Mum and dashed out of the door towards school. It was pouring rain, and she was lucky to have been wearing a long raincoat, wellingtons, as well as having an umbrella with her. She mounted her bike and pedalled past the houses on her way and met Mrs Brown standing in her doorway. Their grumpy old neighbour was recently widowed and lived on her own in her sad, run-down house with her evil-looking black cat. Her house looked somewhat spooky.

"Hello, Mrs Brown", she shouted so the old lady would hear her and also faked a waving hand at her, trying to be polite. But the old lady wasn't in the mood to greet her, just as Ellie wasn't in the mood to confront her. Mrs Brown either hadn't seen Ellie, or she was just so good at pretending not to have done so. Mrs Brown hated children and didn't have any of her own. Ellie didn't care and strode off to school.

At the school gate, Ellie met Charlotte. She went towards her, waving in her direction. "Hey, Charlotte! Good morning."

"Oh, hey Ellie! How're you?" she replied. Charlotte was already drenched by the rain and looked annoyed by that.

"I'm good thanks," said Ellie. Both girls walked hand in hand towards the classroom and chatted easily on their way. They sat at the front desk as usual since Ellie had poor eyesight and had to sit close to the board. They reached into their schoolbags and opened their books. The first hour was mathematics. They were both weak in maths and thus despised it. Pupils were called one by one to go to the board and solve the maths problems. Jane, as always, was good at maths and even asked their teacher if she could solve the next problem, too. She loved to be in the centre of attention and show off her talent. "Miss, can I solve the next one too, please?"

"No, sit down please; it's other's turn. Only one problem each," answered Mrs Rudolf rigidly. "Ellie, you come up to the board, please."

Ellie's heart sank, hammering hard against her chest. She hadn't done her homework and didn't have a single clue what to do. She hesitated for a few seconds. As Ellie stood up in her place to confess that she hadn't filled in her maths worksheet, Charlotte instantly nudged Ellie hard with her elbow and shot her a meaningful look. She discreetly handed Ellie her notebook to save her from a great embarrassment in front of others, since Mrs Rudolf acts relentlessly with lazy students who don't do their homework. She would shout at them or have them do more homework as punishment. Ellie stepped towards the blackboard and picked up a white chalk from beneath the board. Her hands were sweaty, and she was nervous to write from Charlotte's notebook, hardly making out her messy handwriting. She brought her round spectacles to her eyes to have better vision. Luckily, she managed to write down everything correctly and received Mrs Rudolf's satisfied looks. Thanks to Charlotte for helping her again.

After a tedious one hour, the bell finally rang for break time. Ellie and Charlotte rushed out towards the playground. The girls shared their snacks; they enjoyed them better that way. They were like sisters and were almost inseparable and could depend on each other. They did many activities together and were becoming better friends over time. "Oh, I really hate Jane! I wish she wasn't in the class," said Ellie.

"So do I," replied Charlotte.

The next hour was reading time. They could go to the library and choose a book. Ellie and Charlotte entered the library hall. They were both young kids with big dreams. For a moment, Ellie came up with an idea and explained it to Charlotte when they were safely out of earshot.

"Are you stupid? But don't you think it would be too risky to do such a thing, Ellie? I'm not quite sure it'll work out."

"Don't you see? This could be our golden opportunity! Don't be afraid, Charlotte, it won't hurt. We'll try it at least and see where that goes." But Charlotte's gut feeling told her they shouldn't do this and so she shook her head in disagreement with Ellie. Convincing her was harder work. Yet before she refused entirely, Ellie tried once more.

"Come to think of it this way, Charlotte, we might find the very book which will turn our lives in a much better way and make us rich! We should give it a go. I don't suppose it'll cause us trouble this once."

Charlotte was still sceptical about the plan working out but agreed with Ellie, regardless of her unpleasant gut feelings.

All at once, they gently tiptoed the other direction in the library, which was only for teachers' use. They both agreed on finding a book that could show them how to make a lot of money in a short time. So, they searched through various book sections for the relevant title. Some books were placed on the higher shelf levels, which prevented them from even looking at the titles.

"Uh-huh, this must help," whispered Ellie while pointing to a thick hard covered book which was entitled 'Ten Ways to Become Rich'. "I must read this book and take some notes to apply. This should do the trick!"

Then Ellie suddenly looked hopeless and turned to Charlotte. A wave of despair hit her. "*Errrr...* Charlotte, do you have any idea how I should carry this book out without being noticed?" she asked Charlotte thoughtfully while scratching her head and narrowing her eyes.

"*Shh...* keep your voice down or they'll hear us," hissed Charlotte, shooting Ellie a worried look. "I don't know, maybe just grasp it off the shelf and hide it under your jacket," suggested Charlotte, unsure what else to say.

"Okay so let's do it. It won't take long," said Ellie Nervously. They crossed their fingers, hoping nobody would show up. "Charlotte, perhaps you can talk to the library keeper and busy her in a conversation... it might buy us a bit more time," suggested Ellie.

Ellie's palms were sweaty, and her hands were shaking. It was her first time doing such a thing. She tried her best and stood on her toes to make her height taller since she was a short girl for her age. She stretched her hands as high as she could, trying to reach the book, which was placed on the fourth bookshelf. She succeeded after a few attempts and grabbed the book and clutched it in her fingers and hid it under her clothes in a smart attempt. "*Phew!*" she said, and wiped her sweaty hands on her trousers. Neither of the girls had thought about the consequences. As they were about to disappear from the restricted zone, all of a sudden, they met a set of big emerald-green eyes sneaking up on them. They froze in bewilderment. Their hearts fell in their throats and the book slipped from under Ellie's jacket and dropped on the floor. Ellie's hand went involuntarily to her mouth.

"Well, well, well, what am I seeing here?" said a familiar voice out of the blue, appearing at the most inconvenient moment. She folded her arms across her chest in triumph and smirked slyly. She had caught them off guarded.

Ellie quickly kneeled down to grab the book, but Jane was much quicker and snatched the book away, feeling awfully pleased with herself. "I'm going to tell Mrs Bat," she said with an alarming note in her voice. She had a satisfied smile on her face and brushed her hair off her shoulders.

"I'm going to tell her you were stealing books," Jane said shrewdly as her voice trailed off.

"But we weren't stealing books! You've got all this wrong," they protested back through gritted teeth, trying to justify themselves as anger and nervousness were boiling up inside them.

Jane shot them a smug look and said: "Mrs Bat is the one you should make excuses to, not me, you dumbos." Ellie decided she would hate Jane for her entire life.

Mrs Bat was the school headmaster. She was a nasty person and children disliked her and tried to avoid her as much as possible by not getting into trouble. Ellie and Charlotte exchanged looks with troubled expression on their faces. They already knew they were in great trouble, and both let out a big sigh. Ellie was praying for some sort of escape.

A few minutes later, Mrs Bat emerged with a bitter look on her face. Her jet-black hair was tightly pulled back in a bun and she was wearing her long black suit, as usual. She took a step backwards, stood in front of them, and looked them up and down. She was looking into Charlotte and Ellie's eyes, with hers formed into slits and lips pursed. It felt like she was staring right into Ellie's soul, which made her uncomfortable, and she prickled all over. Mrs Bat pointed out towards them with her long black nails.

Mrs Bat raised a brow and blinked at them in disbelief. "It's you two again! Follow me, the pair of you." She summoned them both to her office with a cold look. Her room was on the ground level, which was quite dark, smelling of cold and earth.

Both girls stumbled to find the right words to say. Ellie licked her dry lips. "But we didn't do anything wrong," protested Ellie in a weak tone. "We only wanted to read the book, which we took off the shelf and return it back to the library," she added helplessly.

"I beg your pardon?" said Mrs Bat, narrowing her eyes. She was less than convinced with her alibi.

"Um... sorry Miss... I didn't mean to be rude or something, but I told you the truth," said Ellie with a voice that was hardly even heard, staring at her feet.

Ellie and Charlotte reluctantly had done as they were

told and followed close behind Mrs Bat to her office with shaky legs. Ellie's legs felt like jelly as she took each step closer. Ellie's cheeks were as red as a beet-root.

"It was all your fault!" Charlotte blamed Ellie, scowling at her. "You came up with the idea in the first place!" Charlotte protested angrily with her arms crossed and her cheeks the colour of red apples.

Ellie lowered her head with shame, looking at the floor while walking and whispered back, "I'm terribly sorry, Charlotte. I didn't mean to get us in trouble. I was very foolish to make such a decision." Ellie paused for a moment then added with furrowed brows, "I didn't think taking a book from there would be that much of a big deal." She glanced down at her shoes. Charlotte remained silent and frowned at her, and avoided looking at Ellie's eyes.

After going to the headmaster's room, they were given detention and were ordered to stay indoors in Mrs Bat's office during break time as a punishment for their misbehaviour. They were to write lines, apologising for their bad manners, and stating they wouldn't repeat it. Ellie felt guilty about what she had done. It was unlike her true personality and, therefore, promised herself not to do such a thing ever again. It taught her a good lesson for the future.

While they were sitting in the office, Jane was watching them through the tall windows and made silly faces at them. Ellie and Charlotte felt humiliated. Ellie couldn't stand it any longer and wished she could punch Jane in the face and get rid of her once and for all. Sitting in there and doing their lines felt like hours. Charlotte burst into tears and sulked with Ellie. Ellie sensed that the slightest offense or misspoken word might lead to an argument between them. Charlotte didn't talk to Ellie anymore and kept quiet for the rest of the day. Until then, they'd never sulked in their two-year-friendship. And right now, Ellie was feeling the inevitable rush of guilt passing over her. She felt shameful and blameworthy, and wished she could turn back the clock and undo her mistake.

When the bell rang at the end of the day, Ellie ran after her friend and reached Charlotte near the school exit, but she found her angry. "Why are you coming after me, following me wherever I go? Leave me alone," said Charlotte and rolled her eyes in annoyance and didn't look back.

But Ellie wrapped her arms around Charlotte and tried to make it up to her. "I'm truly sorry, come on, please don't sulk with me… I didn't mean for it to happen." Ellie was genuinely sorry for making trouble for her friend. But Charlotte avoided her.

"Bye!" replied Charlotte in a calm, cool manner. With that, Charlotte turned her back to Ellie and rode off home on her bike. Ellie said nothing in response. She felt like a loser.

The sky was gloomy. Luckily, the rain had stopped pouring, and there were only small raindrops falling from the sky. Ellie's heart broke as she watched with a mixture of disappointment and anger at her best friend pedalling fast down the road until she was totally out of sight. She didn't expect this behaviour from Charlotte. *She won't go without me. She will be back in a few minutes,* Ellie told herself. But as the minutes passed, she realized Charlotte's not returning. Ellie felt a lump grow in her throat, swallowing hard, fighting back tears. She stood there and released a deep, sad sigh, and stamped her feet in the puddle. The water splashed on her skirt, but she didn't care. *It was a miserable Monday*, she thought and rubbed her face wearily.

After a few minutes of standing there, she took her bike and instead of sitting on it, she walked it home. She strolled along the sidewalk towards home with her bike beside her, shoulders slouched, taking heavy-footed steps and dragging her feet while being distracted by her thoughts. It was a crappy day for her at school.

Ellie arrived home an hour later. Her body was droopy, holding a slouched posture, feeling emotionally fatigued. Mum had been waiting for Ellie, sitting on a stool behind the window looking out, feeling anxious for Ellie's delay in coming home, constantly looking at her wristwatch and feeling nervous as the minutes passed by.

DIIING! Ellie appeared behind the front door and rang the doorbell. Mum opened the door in a few seconds. She quickly reached out her hands towards Ellie, hugged her and kissed her daughter on her cheeks and let her in. "Hello darling" said Mum, looking at Ellie with scrutiny. "Why did you come so late? What is the matter, dear? Is everything all right with you?" asked Mum, who seemed to notice the sad look on Ellie's face.

"Hi Mum… Yeah I'm fine… just a bit tired… if I get some rest, I'll feel better," she lied, although she never was a good liar and her body language was always a dead giveaway. She was hoping her Mum couldn't read her mind. Ellie simply forced a smile and tried to sound as casual as she could.

"But I sense you're not as happy as you are other days. What's that you got to feel so glum about?" Mum said with a meaningful look as she let Ellie in and closed the door.

"*Um…* actually I fell out with Charlotte today and she wouldn't talk to me anymore," said Ellie, but it wasn't the entire truth.

Mum furrowed her brows being curious. "Oh, darling, why? What happened between you two?" When she understood Ellie wasn't keen on telling the story, she just left the question there. "Never mind dear, I'm sure you'll work things out together, okay?"

Ellie avoided eye contact with her Mum for the fear of her finding out about what she'd done at school and be cross with her. Instead, Ellie went to pick up the television controller, sat down on the sofa and turned on the TV.

Mum had baked them a delicious apple pie. The sweet, mouth-watering aroma had filled the whole house. "*Yummy*, what a lovely smell, Mum. You're the best cook ever!" said Ellie.

"Thanks, that's a nice compliment, Ellie. Now go wash your hands and come eat at the kitchen table," said Mum with a happy smile.

Ellie's mood brightened up a bit. She was starving and hadn't eaten anything since noon, and eating would refresh her, making her feel much better. She went to the bathroom, washed her hands and went upstairs to her room and changed into her comfortable striped pyjamas, then ran back downstairs to the kitchen to eat their special treat.

"*Mmm…* this is *so* yummy I want to eat it all up," Ellie said as she devoured the apple pie.

After they finished eating, Ellie felt guilty and told her Mum all about the day's incident at school. First her Mum scolded Ellie and then she explained to her calmly that taking something without someone's permission is a very wrong thing to do, especially from a restricted area in a school library. "You must respect and follow the school rules, Ellie. That is very important to keep in mind, and not only school, but any other place you enter." Ellie felt bad about herself, and Mum gave her a hug to calm her. "That's okay, you never learn until you make mistakes and that's part of human nature," said Mum while flicking hairs out of Ellie's face and kissing her on the forehead.

Ellie was in her room sitting behind her desk, too busy with painting a picture on a piece of white paper. While she loved painting, she was fond of all sorts of art. She was painting a picture of a brown horse in a race. She had an original photo of it cut out from a magazine in front of her and was trying to paint it the same. Her room was so cold that she couldn't feel her hands anymore. They had to call the window repair service to come and fix her broken window, which was shattered by a very strong wind during the thunderstorm. She stood up and lit a huge candle, placed it on the desk close to her to keep her hands warm until she finished her painting.

They served dinner around seven o'clock that night. They had chicken breast and boiled potatoes with beans, which they both loved. Ellie was starving, and her stomach was rumbling. She hadn't eaten since the apple pie she had shared with her Mum before four o'clock. So, she gobbled up all the food on her plate in only a few minutes and left nothing on the plate.

She went to bed earlier than usual and picked up a book to read before sleeping. It was a funny book that made her laugh heartily, which was a good distraction for her, making her forget all about her bad day. After reading, she set her book aside and turned off the lights, said good night to her Mum and climbed into her bed. In the first ten minutes, she fluffed the pillow constantly and changed position, unable to doze off. After a while, the tiredness weighed down her eyelids, and she drifted off to sleep followed by occasional snoring sounds. She snored loudly.

CHAPTER FIVE

I t was midnight. Ellie was already fast asleep when her Mum sat down in her rocking chair to sew a red velvet dress. She was trying her best to put away some money for Ellie. But unluckily she had lost some of her customers in the recent weeks since they preferred to buy their clothes from shops during big sales rather than spending more money and time on tailored clothes. She was desperate to find more customers. She perceived that if she didn't find any more soon, she wouldn't be able to save much, alongside paying the bills and other expenses which she had to manage single-handedly to make ends meet.

But Mum kept it to herself and didn't tell her daughter about their poor financial situation. She didn't want to disappoint her. *Ellie is too young to worry about this stuff now*, she told herself. *I should handle this and figure things out by myself*, she admitted. She sank back in the rocking chair, letting out a sigh. For almost an hour, she sat cross-legged, sunk in thoughts. She was lucky for having the house for themselves and shouldn't have to pay a mortgage or rent, at least.

◆ ◆ ◆

The next day, Ellie woke up and dressed for school. On the way to school, Ellie hoped Charlotte would come to her as always with a big hug and cheerful smile. But as she got close to the school railings, she spotted Charlotte, who acted cold, dismissing Ellie and walking inside the school building hand in hand with another classmate named Kiara.

"Charlotte!" called out Ellie desperately, but Charlotte didn't say anything nor even turn back. Ellie felt hot in the face by the rush of blood flow caused by her anger. *How could she be so mean?* Wondered Ellie.

When Ellie entered the classroom, she saw Charlotte sitting next to Kiara. She was in a deep conversation with her, avoiding Ellie, which made her even more furious and jealous. Ellie sat at her usual desk, wishing her friend was sitting next to her and looked downhearted. Even during break times, Charlotte went to the playground with Kiara and Ellie was left with no friend to accompany her. She watched children playing happily in the yard in groups of three or four, having fun while she was standing alone with no one to join her. Ellie felt even more lonely than before and as she stood in a corner of the yard, she kicked hard on the wall beside her. "Ouch!" she cried. She hurt her toes and instantly held her right foot in her hands, limping on her left foot to a nearby bench and sitting.

The weekdays continued the same way. Ellie badly missed Charlotte's presence and could feel her absence. She missed going out together after school making kites or going to the park laughing hysterically on the swings as their hairs were strewn around in their faces in the windy weather.

For weeks after, Jane had been going on in the class about Ellie and Charlotte stealing the book from the library and making nasty jokes about them behind their backs, calling them *thieves* to make her friends laugh during the break time. Jane's stupid friends laughed hysterically at things she said that were not funny.

It wasn't until the next Monday, a day before Charlotte's birthday, when Charlotte spoke to Ellie again. Charlotte had kept quiet for most of the past week. They were at school when Charlotte tapped on Ellie's shoulder and sat next to her in the class. "Hey Ellie, how're you?" she patted on Ellie's back tentatively.

Ellie only shrugged her shoulders, pretending she hadn't heard her and took her book out of her schoolbag. From the corner of her eye, Ellie saw Charlotte reaching into her bag and pulling out an envelope. She reached out her hand towards Ellie. She handed Ellie one of her birthday invitations. Ellie didn't take the envelope from her. There was an uncomfortable silence between them. Ellie had planned to be cross with Charlotte for leaving her alone that day and for avoiding her since.

"Look, I'm very sorry Ellie. I know I let you down so badly that day… and I confess I was acting stupidly in the past few days, but you know, I couldn't hide my feelings because I was cross with you and wasn't exactly in the best of moods," Charlotte explained to her honestly. She added, "Anyway, I wanted to invite you to my birthday party tomorrow. I would love to have you come over, so will you come? Please?" she pleaded, looking into Ellie's eyes. Charlotte had become very chatty trying to make an effort and wanted to fix things between them.

"Why don't you sit with Kiara and invite her instead of me, Charlotte?! I think I don't fit in, and you better spend your precious time with those who are more important to you than me," replied Ellie instantly.

Charlotte knew how Ellie was upset with her and her hopes weren't high for her to be friends again so abruptly. "I understand how cross you are with me Ellie and I give the right to you," said Charlotte, looking ashamed of how she had made her best friend heartbroken. She hesitantly nudged Ellie. "Come on Ellie, please. Let's be friends again, agree?" said Charlotte. She leaned over and kissed Ellie on her head and warmly embraced her best friend, giving her a tight hug. Ellie turned to look at Charlotte then and managed a half-smile, however still avoiding her eyes and kept her face down looking at her shoes.

"I need some time to think about this," said Ellie and busied herself with unzipping her pencil case and arranging her pencils on her desk.

"Okay Ellie, thanks for thinking about my invitation. Just please accept and come, otherwise my party is no fun without you, and you know how important you are to me, don't you?" Charlotte meant her words with all her heart.

"I'll try to be at your party tomorrow if I can, but I can't promise," Ellie answered with reluctance.

"Thank you so much Ellie... I'm sure you will show up and won't let me down."

"I still haven't made up my mind yet," said Ellie quickly.

"I know you will," replied Charlotte with a playful tone and winked at her.

Charlotte had invited nearly all the classmates except Jane. When Jane saw her classmates receiving invitation cards except her, she huffed and called Charlotte names for being selfish and not inviting her.

The next day was an exciting day for kids. It was Charlotte's birthday and her parents had thrown a huge party for her. They had ordered a big Cinderella cake along with a big candle in the middle, which was a number nine, to celebrate. There were colourful balloons everywhere, hanging from the ceilings and some glued to the door or hung on the trees and fences outside their house, which made it look like a wonderland.

Charlotte's parents had hired a big bouncing castle for the kids to play outdoors, as well as a clown and a magician to play shows and entertain children. And there was music playing across the garden. Hopefully, the weather would stay dry as predicted by the weather forecast the night before, and didn't rain for Charlotte's sake.

They had finger foods prepared for the party, along with mini sausages and different sandwiches. There were also fruit juices, coke, lemonade, sweet snacks and chocolates which children enjoyed. Charlotte, as the birthday girl, looked like the star of the show. She was dressed in a stunning, sparkling blue Cinderella costume with an elegant golden crown on her head which emphasised the beauty of her brown hair more than ever. She had her face painted by her mum as a butterfly with glitter glistening all over her glowing honey-complexion. She looked beautiful and adorable and was smiling gracefully at her friends. Charlotte was more than happy to have Ellie at her party.

Ellie had worn a lovely bright purple velvet dress, which her mother had made for her last year and had given it to her as her Christmas gift. She had also painted her nails in a light marshmallow-pink, which suited her outfit perfectly.

Most of Charlotte's friends had joined her party and brought presents for her in all sizes and shapes wrapped up in decorated wrapping paper, which made Charlotte too excited to open them. Eventually, Charlotte opened her gifts and was thrilled to see what wonderful things she was given.

"Ta-dah!" said Charlotte's Mum as Charlotte tore open the paper of the present her Mum and Dad bought her. They got her one of her favourite latest barbie dolls which she had wanted before and had seen it behind a shop's window a while ago. It was a dentist barbie. Charlotte's mouth was wide open and clapped her hands with joy and kissed her mum and dad. She wished to become a dentist in the future and did her best to study hard and get high grades in her lessons.

Ellie had given her a pair of knitted pink gloves with a matching hat and scarf to go with it, which her Mum had knitted. Charlotte became fond of it and thanked her gratefully for the lovely handmade gift.

At the end of the party, Charlotte handed out each person a small party bag containing jelly belly candies, a kinder-surprise, and a small thank-you card. Finally, her friends left their house one by one and said goodbye to her as the sky was growing dark. They all had fun and chatted happily towards home.

Overall, it was a pleasant day for Ellie and she felt joyful in every part. Especially the magic trick part when the magician suddenly pulled out a white rabbit from his black hat only by tapping his wand. She found it very amusing.

CHAPTER SIX

A few days later, while Ellie was pacing the long, clattering school corridors, glancing at the posters and notices pinned on the green, velvet board out of boredom, a particular post caught her eyes. She stepped closer and stared at it for a few seconds. The notice said: 'Be the first-place winner in the running competition and win the prize! Two-hundred pounds for the winner'. It said that the race was going to be held in the schoolyard and it was taking place in a week. Ellie carefully studied the date on the bottom of the post and figured out the poster was posted a week earlier. Therefore, only one week was left until the race.

An idea suddenly struck Ellie. *What if I train as hard as I can in the coming days and compete for the first place? Then I can win the 200-pound prize and register for the horse-riding course. This is incredible! It will be enough to cover the course fees for one month* She was thinking out loud. Her heart gave a leap from excitement, and she started fantasising about approaching her goal. Charlotte was absent that day, so it was a pity she didn't have her best friend to talk to about the idea.

First off, Ellie needed to go to their P.E. teacher, Mrs Green, and question her regarding the details of the competition. She took the stairs up to the second floor and headed towards Mrs Green's office. Ellie knocked on her door twice. "Come in please, it's open," answered Mrs Green while she was busy stirring her tea with a little plastic stick and biting on a ginger biscuit. Ellie twisted the doorknob and entered her room. Mrs Green was wearing a bright coral Adidas sports T-shirt showing off her muscular body, which she took pride in. Her physique was just what any girl wished for.

"Hello Mrs Green," said Ellie in a low voice.

"Oh, Ellie it's you." She looked up and raised her eyebrow, sounding surprised. Mrs Green gestured for her to sit, pointing toward a chair in front of her. "Have a seat please, Ellie." She smiled encouragingly at Ellie, revealing her brilliant white teeth.

"Sorry for disturbing you drinking your tea," said Ellie as she pulled out the chair from under the table and sat.

"Don't worry, that's okay. No problem at all," Mrs Green reassured her.

"Thank you, Miss. *Errm…* well… actually, I had a question about your recent poster pinned on the board," said Ellie, squeezing her fingers hard.

"Go on, dear, ask what you need to know about it.

I'm here to help you." Mrs Green was a kind-hearted teacher who willingly helped children if she could.

Ellie paused for a few seconds and drew a long breath. "Well... how should I explain it? *Um*, I really need to win the race and need the money, so I want to win it. I needed tips for winning? Could you tell me how do I train since I only have a week left to the race?" she asked as she exhaled deeply. Words seemed to jumble out of her mouth and she sounded somehow silly in front of her. Anyway, Ellie asked what she wanted and got the answer she needed. Mrs Green gave her some helpful tips to do during her trainings.

She added, "Ellie, as I'm well aware of your sports ability and your fondness for running, I'm sure you'll do great if you follow my instructions. So, hope to see you in a week!"

"Thanks! See you next week, Buh-bye!" Ellie came out and left the office happily, flying way towards home. She hadn't brought her bike to school, so she had to go on foot. Happiness and joy were written all over Ellie's face as she set off down the road. Ellie decided she'd practice every day. *I must win the race!*

When she arrived at home and her Mum met Ellie's eyes, she immediately noticed a difference in her mood. She stroked her daughter's sweat-soaked hair and asked, "Hey Ellie, what's up? You look very cheery today. I haven't seen you like this in a long time. It seems like you have some good news, ey?" Mum eyed her suspiciously and hoped she was right.

Ellie told her Mum all about next week's competition and how she wants to practise hard to win the prize. "Mum, I'm going to try as hard as I can and I am sure I'm going to be the winner," Ellie said cheerily.

"That's brilliant news. I hope you'd win it," exclaimed Mum.

That day Ellie was full of energy and couldn't spend her time waiting inside the house. She felt the urge to go outdoors, to run across the streets or through the park. She went straight to her room and opened the chest of drawers, taking out a pair of trainers and running trousers along with a sports jacket. She put them on and hurried down the stairs in a few minutes with her trainers in her hands. She was standing by the front door tying her shoelaces when her Mum saw her.

"Where're you going now Ellie? You've just come back from school."

"I'm going for a running practice, Mum," replied Ellie casually.

"But you can't just go running on an empty stomach. You must eat something first and without that, you can't have enough energy," Mum yelled from the kitchen.

"But I don't feel hungry." Ellie rolled her eyes.

"Then have this first before going out just like that." Mum handed Ellie a glass of milk with some wholewheat digestive biscuits.

"I'm not in the mood to eat now." But she ate them

anyway and then gave her mum a quick kiss before walking outside the door to start her running practice.

Ellie initially started by a few dynamic stretches to warm up, followed by a brisk walk. She had learnt from Mrs Green that this step is crucial in starting any sport and mustn't be skipped. Mrs Green had taught her that doing so will raise the temperature of her muscles, improve the blood flow and help loosen up. Thus, it prevents muscles from being pulled too far and tearing or causing other injuries during the activity. The weather was crisp and clear, while having a lovely cool breeze, which made Ellie's strands of hair fly in the air like red flames. Ellie was in a good mood and only thought of the upcoming competition. She was desperately fighting to win it.

She carried her water bottle with her and drank water consistently, keeping her body hydrated to do well, as instructed. She ran for about two hours. By keeping her breathing steady, she pushed harder and went faster. Cold air bit into her lungs. A thin layer of sweat covered the nape of her neck, which required her to pat it dry with her small towel. Her hair also was damp with sweat. Gradually her legs became tired and her entire body, especially calf muscles, became sore. She reached a point where she couldn't continue any further since she wasn't used to running and her muscles weren't yet strong enough. However, she was good at running during their P.E. lessons. As she pushed through, she fell hard on to the paving slabs.

"*Aahh*!" She quickly got to her feet as some pedestrian passing by held out her arm for Ellie to assist her standing up. Ellie's knees hurt badly and were bruised. She stopped to relax. She exhaled and inhaled deeply. She tried to breathe slowly and evenly.

The sun was setting, and the sky began to get dark. Ellie glanced up and realized how dark it had grown. She crossed the streets as her route curved back towards home. She carried on walking into the evening, while her calves felt heavy and swollen and her muscles burned. Darkness had fallen by the time she reached home. She knocked on the front door and her Mum opened it in a wink as if she'd been sitting behind the door waiting for her. "Oh, thank heavens, Ellie, there you are!" exclaimed her Mum with a sharp tone in her voice. "I've been worried about you!"

"Sorry Mum, but you know I won't go far, and besides, the streets are safe here," replied Ellie casually, justifying herself. Since she was an only child, her Mum worried too much about her and was often overprotective.

Ellie was drained and felt too exhausted to even eat. She dragged herself upstairs to her room and spread her clothes all around on the floor and decided she would tidy them later when she regained her energy. She sat on her bed and closed her eyes. Her eyes felt heavy by the overwhelming effect of the adrenaline pumped into her bloodstream after strenuous exercise, and she instantly fell asleep on her bed.

◆ ◆ ◆

Only two days were left until the competition day and it was fast approaching. The lead-up to the day began feeling more and more stressful. The alarm on the bedside table went off at 8am. Ellie leapt with the beeping sound, rose to her feet and drew the curtains away to let the light in. She looked out her window and caught sight of the depressing, gloomy weather. It was raining cats and dogs. She despised rainy days and knew that she ought to put on her long vinyl raincoat and take her large umbrella with her or she would be soaked to the skin. She couldn't help but wish they had a car.

That day at school, pupils were given 10-pound book vouchers to buy a book from the school bookstore. Children were all chatting enthusiastically together and each deciding on the book they wanted to choose. Ellie was a bookworm and enjoyed spending her free time reading books. She developed the habit of reading since toddlerhood. At the age of one, her parents started reading bedtime stories to her. She found books very entertaining and also a fun way to improve her writing and spelling.

She rummaged through the books which were there for sale. Interestingly, she picked up a book which was about 'The World of Animals'. She took a quick glance at the back cover for the price tag, and it was just in the price range as the voucher they were given. Without hesitation, she chose her book and handed the voucher to the saleswoman. Now she had a new book to engage her during her break times, especially those wet rainy days where she had to stay indoors. She was very satisfied with her purchase and couldn't wait to read it during her calm time.

During the break, Ellie and Charlotte reached a quieter section of schoolyard and they both sat on a bench, which was still damp from the morning rain, and showed their books to each other. Each was proud of what they'd chosen. They both chose books by the covers at first. The more colourful the cover was, the more interesting it seemed to them. Charlotte had chosen a tin-tin comic book that appealed little to Ellie. Unlike her, Charlotte had a passion for reading comics.

Ellie had already mentioned to Charlotte about the running competition the same day she had seen the poster. She had even asked Charlotte's opinion if she was interested in joining the race as well, which Charlotte had replied, "no way!" Charlotte hated to run since it only worsened her knee pain. Charlotte had badly fallen off a tree swing at her grandmother's country-house when she was six. The incident had caused a severe fracture in her kneecap, which had resulted in an operation. The flashback of the memories came to Charlotte all at once. Those painful days which she had spent at the hospital in agony, suffering the pain in her right knee. The days where she wore a leg brace and had to walk with the assistance of a walking-stick to have extra support to her leg. The surgeon had strongly advised her against putting pressure on her knee.

CHAPTER SEVEN

It was time to go home and kids happily burst out of the classroom towards the building exit, screaming and laughing with bliss. That day, Charlotte's Mum was supposed to come to the school to pick them up. Mrs Melton was driving her own car. It was an old two-door white Renault which belonged to her husband at first, and was later possessed by her after buying their second car. Recently, it had become irritating and unnerving. The clutch was functioning poorly and causing trouble for her now and then.

She parked in front of the school gates, where the kids could spot her easily among the crowd. There were too many cars on the street belonging to parents awaiting their children, causing heavy traffic on the main street. Charlotte's Mum was very lucky to find a good parking space. She had come twenty minutes earlier than expected. She was an incredibly punctual woman who preferred to show up at least ten minutes earlier than planned and always be on time.

She heard a familiar voice calling her from a close distance and turned towards it. "Hello Mrs Melton!" It was Ellie waving her hands excitedly amid the crowd of pupils in the distance to be seen by her as they walked down the path towards her car.

"Hello Ellie!" Charlotte's Mum yelled back from the car window and waved back her hand at Ellie. She then turned on the car and the engine came to life. She leaned over and opened the passenger door so kids could climb in quickly. The children gladly walked to the car and sat, with Charlotte sitting at the front and Ellie in the backseat. And they drove off towards home with the girls busy speaking about their day at school and expressing the activities they had done.

"How was your day at school, girls?" asked Charlotte's Mum looking at Ellie through her rear-view mirror and smiling at her. She was happy that Charlotte had found herself a good friend at school. Ellie was always so calm and also amusing, so it was hard not to like her.

"Today was great! They gave us each a voucher to buy a book." Ellie proudly took out her book from her schoolbag, excited to show it to Mrs Melton. They jumped up on the speed bumps, which made them giggle. On their way, they passed by a popular ice-cream shop named Gelato. It caught their attention and made their mouths water. Their car stopped at a red light. The girls craved ice cream as they saw some people eating them. Mrs Melton couldn't resist the look on the girls' faces and she agreed to get them an ice cream. "My treat. We'll go have one. How does it sound?" Charlotte's Mum turned around to look at Ellie and winked at her playfully. She was always being affectionate towards Ellie since she was an orphan and didn't have a father.

"*Hurray*!" the girls roared delightedly in unison and clapped their hands. They couldn't wait to have their ice cream. Ellie had a sweet tooth and a strong fondness for sweet stuff. She often craved to have something sweet like cakes and chocolates to fulfil her, rather than salty or sour things. But her Mum had set boundaries for her, prohibiting her from eating too many sweets. This had become the rule in their house. She could only eat a certain number of sweets per day and mustn't exceed it.

So off they went towards the ice-cream shop. Charlotte's Mum grabbed their arms protectively as the three of them crossed the road. They reached the ice-cream shop, and the girls gazed eagerly at the heavenly chocolaty and fruity ice-cream scoops, and they drooled. "I fancy a Chocolate Cookie flavour," said Ellie with such excitement.

"And I love a strawberry-flavour scoop," added Charlotte.

All three of them, including Charlotte's Mum, chose theirs to have in a cone and went inside the shop and found an empty table to sit. Ellie's favourite spot was to sit by the window where she could see outside and watch people walking on the pavement. They began licking and biting on their ice creams impatiently. Ellie had brown smears all around her mouth and the tip of her nose as the result of digging into her ice cream, which made Charlotte and her Mum laugh. She then watched herself in the mirror and chuckled, too. She asked for a tissue to clean the mess on her face.

Later, when they finished eating, they went back to the car. Just after four o'clock, the little white car pulled up in front of Ellie's Mum's house. Ellie's mum stood at the front door.

"Good afternoon, Mrs Melton. Thanks a lot for picking Ellie up from school today. Would you like to come in for a cup of tea?" she shouted as she walked to the car.

"Hello Mrs Patterson, no problem at all! Thank you very much. Perhaps I will visit another time," Charlotte's Mum replied, stretching her neck out of the car window. She dropped Ellie off at her house and they said goodbye and she drove off. It was a pleasant day for Ellie.

The next day was the big event. One week had flown by so fast. First thing after coming home from school, Ellie ran upstairs to her room and hastily changed into her running pants and sports jacket and left the house to do her last day of training. She started again by slow walks and movements for warming up every muscle in her body. Then she progressed to run along the park nearby across the group of trees, hearing the laughter and sounds of kids playing football on the grass. By running consistently every day, she had become faster at running and improved a lot compared to her first day of practice, which she found it a positive sign.

After about a good two hours of hard practice, Ellie headed home with sweat dripping down her forehead, knowing that her Mum would expect her before dusk. She could hardly make it to home since she had grown two big blisters on her toes, which hurt a lot. And she was so exhausted that she could hardly put one foot in front of the other. *Oh gosh! Now how am I going to run tomorrow with these blisters?* She hoped they would go away by some miracle.

Ellie hated short winter days and wished it could always be summer with the long, bright, sunny days. The dark, cold, rainy days influenced her mood, causing her to feel down. *Tomorrow, when the competition is all over, I'll be giggling with joy that I've ranked first among the competitors*, she thought.

Her mum had made them some hot popcorn and brought it from the kitchen with her, along with a bottle of freshly squeezed orange juice. "I love popcorn," said Ellie as she stretched her hands and grabbed the bowl of popcorn from her Mum right away. Her Mum mostly preferred home-made foods. In her opinion, they were much healthier, tastier, and also cheaper than buying them from the supermarkets. Ellie shoved handfuls of popcorn in her mouth while she was watching her favourite TV show. After eating and watching TV, Ellie dozed off on the sofa having a quick nap in front of the cartoon programme. Her Mum was busy talking to her but when she didn't hear any response, she then turned her head and realized Ellie was sound asleep. She got up and brought her a warm blanket and covered her.

They had a chimney in their living room. Even so, it felt cold. Her mum shivered, wishing their house was easier to warm up. Their living room was on the ground floor. It was tiny, hardly fitting a couch, a miniature television stand, a small coffee table, and three armchairs. They had an oval navy wool rug on the floor which only partially covered the grey tiles beneath it and left the rest exposed.

Lately, Ellie's mum had also begun knitting clothes beside sewing. She suspected that with just sewing, she could make decent money for a living. Unfortunately, these days, few people were interested in having their clothes tailored for them; People preferred to buy clothes from shops and even more desirable for them was to buy them during the sales seasons for a much lower price. And besides, nowadays with all people, including most women, having full-time jobs, they could hardly find the time for going to a private tailor and being measured with a meter and going back and forth to try out the clothes at least twice. They mainly thought it's a huge waste of time. These all explained the reason for losing her customers day by day. Which was a very sad truth she had to come to terms with.

Meanwhile, Ellie's Mum had sought part-time jobs or maybe – if no other choices left – a full-time job. She had searched through the newspapers for any open job offers. She found some open positions and made a list of them. She applied for a few positions as a tailor in a shop or as a cashier woman at the local supermarkets and some other shops in their district, not very far from their home.

Few weeks passed by and Ellie's Mum was still hoping to receive an answer back, being accepted by any of the jobs she had applied for and filled in the job applications for. To her dismay, she hadn't yet received a single letter from any of the positions she had applied for. She was feeling more nervous and stressed. This was eating at her, and she had no other option but to disguise her sadness from her daughter.

As the days went by, their financial status was becoming far worse than before and Ellie's Mum was left with only a little money. She tried hard to hide her frustration and disappointment from Ellie and act indifferently whenever Ellie was around.

The amount of stress had caused her to grow more and more white hairs on her head. She came up with the decision to put some of their furniture or house stuff for sale. She hated to admit that, but she knew there weren't many options left for her. They had to live on a tight budget and eventually she had to let Ellie know the sad truth and make her prepared for what was ahead.

Her Mum's pride didn't allow her to lend money from a friend or family. Also, she knew well that taking house loans from the bank was another bigger burden on her shoulders. Thus, she totally dismissed the idea.

While Ellie was asleep, her mum preferred to do the laundry in the washing machine, which was hopefully fixed. There was a big pile of unwashed clothes dumped into the laundry basket, waiting to be cleaned. Most of them were Ellie's dirty sport clothes, which she had scattered all around her room after wearing them, and her Mum had to collect them to throw in the washing machine. She loaded the clothes and turned on the machine. Ellie's Mum was a neat and clean lady and did not like the house to be untidy. Afterwards, she started dusting with her all-purpose cleaning cloth. In Ellie's room, her belongings, which were placed on the shelf, had collected a thick layer of dust and were scattered in an unorderly way. She had told Ellie many times to dust her stuff frequently and arrange them in an orderly way, but Ellie just postponed house tasks for later, as usual. *She ought to learn to become responsible at least for tidying her own stuff and organising her own room, if not other places in the house... She is old enough to give me a hand and help me with some housework... I must add new rules to this house*, she muttered to herself trying to stop from going crazy.

It was nighttime; Ellie's Mum had already slept. Ellie was in her room and had changed into her soft pyjamas. She reached towards her window and looked out into the moonlit night. She stood staring at the moon, which had emerged from behind the clouds shining into her room, brightening her room with its silver light. She opened the window and poked her face out and took a deep breath. She stood listening to the sound of rustling tree leaves in the street with the wind. After a few minutes, she shivered and closed the window. Ellie turned out the lights in her bedroom and shut the shutters, blocking out street-lights so she could get adequate sleep for tomorrow's running competition. She pulled the blanket up to her nose, feeling cold, which was mostly because of being stressed out. Her stomach turned over as she thought of losing the competition, mulling it over in her head. Even so, Ellie tried her best to dismiss the idea and remain optimistic instead. She tossed and turned rest-lessly, unable to fall asleep. She snuggled, making her-self comfy and warm. After an hour and a half, she eventually drifted into a fitful sleep, which she woke up now and then.

CHAPTER EIGHT

It was seven in the morning when Ellie woke up feeling uneasy. She was having bad dreams just minutes ago and her forehead was covered with cold sweat. Dark circles had emerged under her eyes overnight, and she felt as if she was awake all night. She had been twisting and turning and hadn't slept a wink. The dream she had was already fading in her mind, and soon she couldn't remember anything about it, not even a single scene of it. But she was sure it was an unpleasant dream. Ellie tried hard to retrieve her memory by pressing her fingers onto her scalp and shutting her eyes, as if it helped her. But it was of no use, and she let go, shoving the dream to the back of her mind. She opened her eyelids, her eyes felt heavy. Ellie stared across the room at the faint light in the window coming from between the shutters, blinking rapidly, remembering it was "The Big Day." She had a premonition that something bad would happen but didn't know what exactly. Her gut feeling ensured her about it. Boom… boom… boom! Her heart was pumping incredibly fast, as if it were about to jump out of her chest. She was fully awake now and slipped out from under the covers, pulled her robe around her shoulders and was on her feet in an instant. She moved with bare feet, tiptoeing down the stairs to drink some water as not to wake her mum up.

Ellie was stepping on the second stair when the phone suddenly rang and startled her. She watched Mum swiftly rush out of her room in her striped sleeping gown to pick the phone up quickly, hoping it wouldn't awaken her daughter. A third ring, and she fumbled for the receiver and grabbed it. "Yes, hello," she said as she sat on the armchair nearest the telephone. She was listening carefully to the person on the other side of the phone.

"Good morning, sir. Yes, that's me, sir," Mum replied immediately. Ellie could tell by the formality of the voice that it was someone calling from the hospital or the police station. She felt her anxiety was growing. It was Doctor Evan Davidson on the other side of the phone.

"Oh no, what about my mother? What's happened to her?" The words came out angrier than she'd intended. Her hands were trembling uncontrollably and were as cold as ice, waiting for his response.

Ellie was eavesdropping by standing very close to the living room, hiding behind the wall. She was hearing her Mum speaking into the phone.

It took a moment for Mum's brain to catch up what she was hearing. "Oh! my goodness, she's had a cardiac arrest minutes ago? How's that possible?" she panicked, her face white as chalk and her voice weak.

Mum dropped the phone onto the floor when she learned that her mum had passed away a few minutes earlier. She muttered to herself breathlessly, "this can't be true… this can't be true… I'm hallucinating…" She was going to faint and the room around her seemed to spin nonstop.

Although she was well aware that lately her Mum had been feeling poorly, they hadn't taken it very seriously. The skin around her Mum's eyes was dark and tired and her cheeks weren't as plump as they used to be.

Mum could hardly hear the doctor's voice. She instead demanded, "which hospital should I come?" Her voice was tight and pained. She hardly jotted down the name and address of the hospital as the doctor was telling her and then she hung up the phone and left it hanging from the table.

"She CANNOT be dead! This can't be real!" murmured Mum while resting her head gently on the wall behind her as if trying to support herself from falling.

Ellie was awestruck and was staring at her Mum and the phone without blinking, unable to take a single step. She was baffled and overwhelmed by what she'd just seen and heard from her Mum, and tried to figure out what had really happened, but was too afraid to even go further and ask her Mum. But what she learned from her Mum's conversation was that someone had died, that was for sure.

Who had died? Who could it be? The questions were forming in Ellie's head, one after the other. She walked towards her mum, neared the telephone, which was a brown, old-fashioned one, and put the hanging handset back on its cradle. Every minute seemed like an eternity for Ellie, while waiting for her mum to tell her the bad news.

Mum told Ellie that her Grandma had passed away. Ellie just sat on the ground staring at the wall in front of her with a deep sorrow. "Oh, my God!" said Ellie. A piercing shriek echoed through the house then. Ellie felt light-headed and dizzy, which was triggered by the sudden shock she experienced. It caused her to sink down onto the steps next to her, holding her hand on the staircase. She couldn't believe it and thought she was having a nightmare. Every single minute was passing with an agonizing slowness for Ellie, and she was experiencing it with every cell of her body.

Silence fell in the house, apart from the ticking sound of the living room clock. Ellie and her Mum both sat next to one another and held each other firmly. Ellie threw herself into her Mum's embrace and leant against her chest. She listened to her Mum's heartbeat. She had a feeling that if she didn't grasp her Mum hard enough, she might also lose her and have no one else in this world.

They began weeping and sobbing, releasing the deep

emotional pain they suffered from. Mum wiped Ellie's tears dabbing at her eyes with a tissue and tried to soothe and console her. She put a hand on Ellie's chin and gently tilted her head up. "My dear, don't you worry. Your grandma is in the best place ever. She's in Heaven now and is watching us with a big smile on her face, even though we can't see her," she said between sniffs and sobs. "She is resting in peace and is surely satisfied and happier with her place she is now... One day, every single one of us will have to go from this world, sooner or later. None of us are going to live forever. This is the unavoidable fact... it's the way life works and we should accept our fates." She tried to be strong, and calmed Ellie, putting on a brave face and tried to remain logical. Ellie calmed down a little by her Mum's words and began hiccupping. She blew her nose into the tissue and with the help of her Mum she got to her feet and went to wash her face in the sink under the cold running water.

Ellie was all too aware that she'd already lost the running competition despite the week of hard practice she had performed to succeed and win the race.

Mum and Grandpa had to arrange a funeral service for the following day. They also made some phone calls for telling the bad news to their close relatives and informing them about the funeral ceremony. Ellie feared death. She was feeling miserable and looked pale. She began crying again. Losing her grandma was too much of a shock for her to absorb and digest at the moment. It reminded her of her dad's sudden death.

Even though she was too little to remember many details, she still had some vague memories of his death and the time at which her Mum was in a state of melancholy and deep depression, where her grandma had to take care of them. Ellie had all these bad memories accumulated in her subconscious memory. And now this anguish and shock had brought back those feelings. Reminiscing about those events pained her. She was shaking while weeping and felt cold. Her Mum urged her to have something to eat. Her blood pressure had dropped since she hadn't had anything since last night.

Meanwhile, at school, it was ten past nine and Mrs Green was already present in the running field amongst all the pupils who had taken part in the competition. She was wearing a pair of white trainers and her black Adidas track suit and carried a sports bag over her right shoulder. She looked at her wristwatch to check the time.

There were thirty-four competitors in total who had registered their names on the list of runners. After ten minutes, Mrs Green got a weird sense in her gut that one person was missing among them. So, she pulled the list of names out from her pocket. She blew in her whistle and told the pupils to all gather in a close circle around her so she would call their names and check everyone's name off and make sure they were all present. At the end of the list, she got to Ellie's name and read her name out loud, "Ellie Patterson?" No reply, so she realized she's absent. Mrs Green waited a good ten minutes in the hope of Ellie showing up, but she didn't.

They had to start the race at nine-thirty and only ten more minutes were left. She grew worried and anxious for Ellie since she knew how desperately she wanted to join the race and win the prize. She found it mysterious that Ellie hadn't shown up. Mrs Green marched off into the main school building and thought it was best to first make a phone call to her home and ask her Mum the reason for her not turning up. Maybe she is sick or maybe she's had an accident on her way. She should find out, she thought.

She pulled out the files with pupils' addresses and telephone numbers written in it. She swiftly scanned through the list of students' names in alphabetic order, found Ellie's profile, and pulled it out. She walked to the office telephone, picked up the receiver, and dialled the numbers. It was ringing, and she was nervously waiting for someone to pick up the phone. As she was about to hang up the phone on the fifth ring, she heard a weak, shallow voice at the other end saying, "Yeah, hello?"

Mrs Green pulled herself together and hesitantly answered back in a not-so-calm tone, "Hello, is this Mrs Peterson, Ellie's Mum I'm talking to?"

She heard a slight coughing and sniffing sound, "Yes, yes, that's right It's me. Is anything the matter?" Her sound was quite coarse and seemed as if she was sorrowful or had cried.

"I'm sorry if I disturbed you," she cleared her throat and continued, feeling a little uneasy. "I'm Mrs Green, Ellie's P.E. teacher. As you may be aware of, today we are holding a school running race and Ellie was supposed to be here in the running field already. May I ask why she hasn't shown up yet? Has anything happened to her?"

"Oh, uh… yes, yes, of course I'm aware of her race today. But unfortunately, she found out about her beloved grandmother's sudden death a while ago and she's in a big shock and a bad status at the moment." Mum's voice seemed shaky, as if she was about to cry at any minute. "Sadly, she cannot come to the race anymore."

Mrs Green gasped, upset by what she'd just heard. "Oh my god, I'm deeply sorry to hear about the loss of your mother. I can't imagine how you must be feeling right now. Please accept my sincere condolences and send much love to Ellie." *Poor girl*, she thought.

They started the race without Ellie at the scheduled time. Eager to win the race, the competitors ran fast and furious in the field. After thirty minutes of running around the field, the first three winners passed the finish line, with only a few seconds' difference between each of them. The first-place winner, who won the two-hundred-pounds prize, was a girl in their class named Laura. Laura was a competent runner and had trained very hard for the race. She was a huge fan of sports. She had an athletic body and was a really fast runner. Mrs Green felt a pity for Ellie not being able to win the prize, but also thought to herself that if she were there, the chances were slim to beat Laura. Since Laura had been awarded a few running competition certificates for becoming the first in their school and was known as 'the girl who is as quick as a lightning'.

By noon, Ellie felt dazed and went for a long walk in the streets to have some time alone, shaking off the grief. By the time she got home, she found Charlotte and her Mum had come to their house to console them with a big bouquet and had prepared some warm meal for them to eat that night. "Thanks a lot. And sorry for putting you in trouble, it's very thoughtful of you," said Ellie's Mum.

"Oh, not at all, don't worry... By the way, I can also help you with the funeral stuff; just tell me if there's anything I could do," said Charlotte's Mum being very kind and helpful to them.

"I think me and Dad will manage just fine. Thank you for offering anyway," replied Ellie's Mum.

That night Ellie slept with her Mum in her bed to feel her next to herself. They both craved to cuddle each other, and lend support to one another. This way, they could comfort each other and empathise. Mum turned off the light and crept into the bed next to her daughter. She was trying her best to remain strong and supportive for Ellie but was finding it quite hard. Mum looked somewhat thinner and more fragile by night. They had to get as much sleep as possible since the next day they had to go to the hospital's morgue to claim grandma's corpse for burial, and after that, arrange the funeral service.

Ellie's mind was spinning, and she felt dizzy, knowing it would be ages before she fell asleep. As they talked for a while and cried, Mum's eyelids slowly closed and she dozed off quickly because of the sleeping pills she had taken earlier, and started snoring. As Ellie had anticipated, she stayed up till three in the morning, and cried uncontrollably for losing her loving grandma, with her head dug inside her pillow. She was thinking of the nice memories they had together, over and over in her head. She looked out of the bedroom window, spotting a young man sitting on a short wall singing to himself without a care in the world, as if he had no worries in his life. She wished she too could be indifferent about things the same as the man.

CHAPTER NINE

Over the next few weeks, Ellie missed her grandma terribly. With all the bad events which had happened during the past week, she was feeling depressed and was silent, which was unusual for someone like her who was talkative at home. She locked herself in her room for hours and had no appetite or the slightest desire to eat anything. Her Mum asked her what she wanted for supper but she was feeling too unwell to eat. "But darling, you must be starving by now," her Mum told her from behind her closed door. Mum would put the food tray behind her door, but Ellie would leave her plate untouched. "Poor thing, she must be starving," her mum whispered under her breath, but she knew deep down that there was only so much a child of this age could tolerate. Ellie had become more jittery than usual. Ellie had totally lost faith in good things happening to her and thus, lost hope to continue following her dreams. She felt utterly hopeless.

One day when she was in her room, she lost her temper and yelled out loud, *"Believe in good things! Believe in miracles! Go after your dreams!* They're all bunch of crap which everyone tries to teach us!" She threw her books and school stuff on the ground, taking her anger out on them. She was finding it very hard not to be pessimistic. The unfortunate events had weighed her down.

Her literature teacher, Mrs Brook, had advised them, "Don't adopt a negative belief, because then you will attract negative situations." Ellie was struggling to feel positive and change her mood, and didn't want to try anymore. She had given up already. And even had second thoughts about wanting to become a horse-rider. She thought it wasn't worth trying for.

When her grandma was alive, she used to tell her stories about heroes or great ambitious people in history who had made big successes in their lives and how they had never given up on the worst of days. Ellie was touched by these stories, which were the motivational fuel for her to keep going on, no matter what obstacles and barriers she might face in life. "Never worry too much or get too worked up. Everything will sort itself out," she used to say time and again, reassuring her granddaughter. Grandma used to tell her that a world of mystery and wonder awaits. To Ellie, her Grandma was a person anyone needed, not only at hard times, but always. It was a pity she didn't live any longer amongst them, which tore Ellie's heart. "You always listen to my words Ellie, but never understand what I am telling you and you never apply it in your life. Once, give it a try."

Ellie recalled one Sunday afternoon when she was at her Grandma's, her grandma was telling her, "If you want to be a horse-rider and you want it badly, then no one can take it from you. Do you understand Ellie? And remember that even the most famous people in the world have created their dream life from scratch."

But the problem was that Ellie never had faith in herself despite the many stories her grandma read to her or however many positive quotes she read. Still, deep down in her heart, Ellie believed she couldn't get what she wanted because she wasn't made for achieving goals, let alone big goals, and these things were meant for the real strong people, not ordinary and poor people like her.

◆ ◆ ◆

One bright Monday morning, the phone rang, making Ellie's Mum jump out of her bed. She had to clear her throat before answering it.

"Hello?"

"Hello, is this Mrs Peterson?"

"Yes, that's me."

"Perfect! I am calling you from the 'Clothes for all' boutique, wanting to let you know you are accepted for this job, and you suit us well to work here."

Mum was so grateful to hear that she was accepted for one job she had applied to weeks ago and she had to work as a tailor in one shop close to their home.

It was a small boutique named 'Clothes for all' selling women's clothes. They required an experienced tailor who could change the size or length of the clothes according to the customer's preference. This was something which she had the skills for and was experienced in. She felt wonderful working there.

They asked her if she could come to their place the same day and do the paperwork and sign the contract so she could officially start her work the following week. They offered her a monthly salary of 900 Pounds, which was fine for her, and she agreed.

Mum couldn't wait for Ellie to come back from school and tell her the good news and celebrate it together. She felt relieved and as if a heavy burden was taken off her back.

◆ ◆ ◆

After a few weeks, Ellie's life began going on as normal again. It was a dull rainy afternoon when Ellie just lay lazily on the sofa in front of the telly, stretching her feet out in front of her. She wore her extra warm pyjamas with the snoopy prints all over them, flicking through a Horse magazine, skimming it from cover to cover.

At the same time, she was watching the Top Chef cookery programme, when she came up with an idea that hatched in her head in just a few seconds. She felt a rush of hope pass through her heart and smiled satisfyingly to herself. She got up and went to find her Mum who stood by the oven in their little kitchen. She was already busy baking banana cake for their tea-time. Mum always made low-sugar and low-fat cakes for them in order to be healthier. Mum's banana cakes were the best. Once you started, it was impossible to stop eating them!

"*Mum!*... I think I found a way for making extra money by myself." She was trembling with excitement. She had never felt more alive.

"Oh really? and what's that?" her Mum asked with a smile on her face, eyeballing her, unsure of what her daughter had come up with.

"Well... um... I watched this programme about making muffins now," she started, while taking a seat on a white plastic chair.

"Okay, so?"

"I was thinking about learning to make muffins with that special recipe of Grandma's and I could sell it to Mrs Todd at her Bakery just across the street."

Years ago, Ellie's Grandma was popular for her delicious muffins, which were made with a special recipe which she had come up with by herself, and you couldn't find a similar tasting muffin at the shops. Grandma worked in a confectionary shop years ago when she was still young and full of energy. She knew how to make different cakes and pies and especially how to make exquisite and appetising muffins with blueberry filling or chocolate or nuts. She had passed on the recipes and also the talent to her daughter and now Ellie's Mum had the notebook in her hand.

"But Ellie, you have to focus on your homework and your school lessons at the moment, dear. You're already weak in your maths and other lessons and you know that yourself."

"Let me first give it a try. *Please, Mum*?" said Ellie, begging her Mum.

"Okay... Okay... then first you should promise me you won't let it take much of your studying hours and hurt your grades. And you must finish doing your homework then you do that stuff, agreed?"

"Okay... I promise. I would do my homework first and try not to be distracted by the baking thing." Ellie tried to talk her mum into it and convince her. With that, Ellie got to her feet and made her way upstairs to her room. She pulled open the drawer beside her desk and rummaged through the disorderly contents, trying to find what she was looking for. She then hit upon a solid object, lay her fingers on it and grasped the pink porcelain piggy bank. She felt pleased and settled it on her desk. It was given to her by her granny for Easter, along with chocolate eggs. It had never occurred to Ellie to use it, which explains why it was tossed in there amid a pile of other unused objects covered in a thick layer of white dust. She wiped it clean with a wet cloth, placed it on her table and stood staring at it. She took a piece of masking tape from the drawer and wrote on it with a felt-tip pen: **A penny saved is a penny earned**. This was a famous saying by Benjamin

Franklin, which she had learned from her Literature teacher. She stuck the masking tape on the porcelain pig.

"Ah-hah perfect! I will make money soon and join a horse-riding club someday." She thought this was a good chance to take her a few steps towards her future goal. Ellie was determined to realize her dream.

CHAPTER TEN

To Ellie's surprise, thankfully, for two weeks after the death of her Grandma, Jane had lost her taste for bullying. Although Ellie had little faith in her attitude, remaining that way for long. They had History lesson in the first hour, which was such a bore to Ellie. History was her least favourite lesson. To her, it felt like torture sitting and listening to all the boring history stories and stuff in the past, all about wars and kingdoms and empires.

The night before, Ellie could hardly sleep, so her eyes were playing tricks on her, making it much more difficult to focus on the teacher's speech, which was about Tutankhamun. Excitement about making and selling muffins had kept her awake this time. She was yawning frequently, barely coping with the subject. In the last half hour, Ellie explained her 'Muffin' idea to Charlotte in the hope of feeling awake, but more importantly, to inform her friend about her latest plan she'd come up with. She patted on Charlotte's shoulder. "Charlotte, I have a new plan. Guess what?" Ellie eagerly whispered so as not to be heard by the teacher.

"I'm happy to hear it. So, what is this plan of yours?" Charlotte whispered back kind-heartedly. She was more than happy for her best friend to come back to her normal self.

Ellie answered with her tone slightly increasing, as if totally forgetting she's in class, "I've planned to bake different muffins at home with the help of my Mum, and go sell them at Mrs Todd's Bakery shop. This way I can have my own pocket money and save it in my piggy bank. It's not my finest idea, but I've run out of any others at the moment. So, what do you think of it?" She grinned widely.

"Wow, cool! I think it works well. This sounds fun to me. I can't wait to see how it goes. I'm sure you'll make the best muffins ever!" She winked in agreement. They were talking in a loud whisper.

"You two! Please stop talking this instant or I'm afraid I'll have you out of the classroom," barked Mrs Hamilton, their History teacher. She peered at them over her glasses. She quickly goes out of control and loses her temper when children talk in the class while she's giving a lecture.

"Sorry Miss," they both said in unison and stared down into their books and remained as quiet as possible till the end of the class. It felt quite embarrassing to become the centre of attention in the class, having other classmates turn to look at them. Especially Jane!

Jane smirked at them, letting out a small snort. Pretending to itch her leg, Jane tilted her head down and ducked behind her front seat classmate and turned her face to them and grimaced by pulling a silly face with both index fingers in her mouth, pulling it apart. She was back to her annoying self again. She had been on her best behaviour until then. Ellie felt a flash of irritation and swallowed down her frustration, trying to keep her cool and to look as unbothered as possible. She opened her mouth, clearly wanting to say something and answer her back, but shut her mouth and remained silent.

After school, on her way back home, Ellie went to Mrs Todd's Bakery first thing before going home. Her bakery was just a few blocks away from their home, on the other side of the street. Ellie hopped and ran all the way there, grinning ear to ear. She sang to herself and threw her arms up and down in the air, breathing the lovely weather. She was more than excited for her plan would work out and hopefully she'll make some decent money out of this job in no time and would save it all. She was tingling with excitement. However, deep in her heart, she had the gut feeling that this idea of hers wouldn't turn out as she expected. But decided to give it a try, anyway.

By the time she reached the Bakery, sweat was dripping down the sides of her face and her hair. All the running she had done had made her feel too hot, despite the fact that it was a cold winter's day.

Next minute, Ellie hopped on the first step of the shop, raised her head high and caught a glimpse of the Bakery's OPEN sign. She felt a surge of happiness. She took a deep breath, hoped for the best, and pushed the glass door open and entered. At a first glance, Mrs Todd was nowhere to be seen, but then she saw the woman come out from the little room inside the shop which was the 'baking room'. She was busy preparing and arranging the trays of cupcakes, pies, and other cakes and hadn't noticed Ellie's presence.

Mrs Todd bent over, lowering her height behind the glass where she displayed her cakes to customers and at the very moment added a big tray of her fresh-baked, hot apple pies, which the smell of those sweet spices and cinnamon filled the shop making Ellie's mouth water. Ellie realized Mrs Todd hadn't seen her yet and thus pretended a polite cough sound to inform her of her presence and to avoid Mrs Todd's sudden shock when she saw Ellie inside the shop.

"Uhum... Uhum." She put her hand in front of her mouth, faking a cough. "Good afternoon, Mrs Todd!" said Ellie. But her voice was too low to be heard amongst the ear-hammering sound of the music play-ing in the background. She raised her voice a second time and nearly shouted, "GOOD AFTERNOON MRS TODD!" Ellie was getting annoyed by the loud music.

Mrs Todd heard her voice and instantly raised her head and stood to her full height, surprised to see Ellie in her shop after a long time. "Oh!" she cleared her throat as she caught sight of her. "Ellie, it's you here! Sorry, I didn't hear you with this music playing loudly right behind my ears." With that, thankfully, she turned down the music volume, which could hardly be heard.

"Long time no see Ellie! I'm very glad to see you here, dear," she honestly was happy to see Ellie, which was evident in her blue sparkling eyes. She knew Ellie since the day she was born. She clearly remembered the day which Ellie's father came into her shop bursting with joy, coming to buy a big cake to celebrate little Ellie's birth on twenty-second of March, a nice warm sunny day in spring. It was a memorable day for Ellie's Mum and Dad, and for her too.

"So, young Ellie, tell me what do you want to buy from here, huh?" By pointing at the trays behind the glass, Mrs Todd suggested, "Today we have apple pies, a blueberry muffin, some pancakes, a chocolate cake, cinnamon rolls, ginger breads". She kept going on about her pastries, which made Ellie uneasy since she'd come for another reason and not for buying cakes.

"No... none of them, I'm afraid, Mrs Todd," Ellie cut her off mid-sentence before she continued listing all thin=gs she had available. "Sorry that I interrupted you but... *err*, to be honest, Mrs Todd, I've come to discuss something with you," explained Ellie. Ellie's voice was shaking a little. Her cheeks slightly blushed, and was pressing her fingers together to calm herself from feeling nervous. Deep down she was feeling nervous if her idea would be rejected by Mrs Todd, and Ellie crossed her fingers in the hope of her suggestion being accepted by Mrs Todd.

"You're a naughty girl. How can you come here and

not buy anything?" joked Mrs Todd and giggled. Ellie let out a nervous chuckle. She obviously wasn't in the mood for jokes. "Well, I'm just kidding dear, to make you laugh, that's okay… that's okay." She laughed re-assuringly as she waved her hands. "Okay, go on then… tell me, what is it you want from me?" She was a soft-hearted, good-natured lady who was overly keen and always eager to help. She had an average height and a round figure with big chubby cheeks which somehow made her even cuter. And always had her white hat and apron on while in her shop. Poor lady was gaining more weight each day and already she almost weighed a hundred kilograms. There was a gap developed between the middle part of her shirt which had caused the buttons on it to burst. The lady had a poor health condition and hormonal imbalance, which led to her gaining weight more easily by eating even a little amount of food.

Ellie took a long, slow breath. "Well… I came up with this idea that if it's possible for you, I make some homemade muffins and bring them to your shop and you sell them for me. To be honest, I need the money and that's why this idea came into my mind, Mrs Todd. You can give a part of the money to me and keep the rest for yourself. If you agree?"

"Aww, I see… well, yes I understand… let me think for a moment and make up my mind, dear," replied Mrs Todd with an understanding look on her face. She was busy thinking and furrowed her brow for a moment, which made Ellie's heart sink, thinking that she wouldn't agree. "Okay dear, deal! I agree." She had a big, warm smile. Ellie stared at her like she hadn't heard her right. Mrs Todd continued, "You should first bring an example of your muffins to me so I'll test them, then if I approve of them in terms of their taste and texture and the appearance, you are welcome to bake a number of them and bring them to my shop for selling them."

By hearing that it gave Ellie a pinch of hope, and her mood lightened immediately. She could barely conceal her delight. Then Mrs Todd added in a lower voice, nearly like a whisper, "I know some of my customers who are a big fan of muffins and come here every single day to buy them. By the way, blueberry muffins and chocolate chip muffins are also in high demand." She honestly advised Ellie.

As soon as Ellie got back home, she told her Mum all about her conversation with Mrs Todd. She begged her Mum to come to the supermarket to do the muffin shopping, buying items needed for baking muffins. Her Mum had a lot of house tasks to finish. "*Please* Mum, just this once? I promise I won't take long, and we'll come back soon so you can do the rest of your work. Or I can give you a hand and help you. *Please*?" Ellie gave her Mum one of those looks which her Mum couldn't resist.

"Okay, okay! You somehow always persuade me into doing you a favour."

CHAPTER ELEVEN

The next day, as soon as Ellie got home from school, she disappeared into her room, doing her homework and finishing it soon so her Mum will let her make muffins, under her supervision, of course. As Ellie sat behind her desk, she first looked outside her room from the window to clear her mind of distractions, catching sight of the moving clouds and listening to the gust of wind. She saw an old man wearing a long grey coat with a brown pork-pie hat on his head, holding on to his papers in his hand clutching tightly, defending against the strong burst of air sending his papers flying into the air. In just a few seconds, his hat flew off his head into a puddle and the wind stirred his hair. Ellie was struck by how strong the wind was outside. Poor old guy, she thought. And went back to her seat and started doing her homework.

It was half past four when Ellie finished doing what she had to do, and she was still very energetic at that time of the day because she was eager for the 'muffin baking time'. She scurried down the stairs and headed straight to the kitchen to find her Mum in there as usual. "Hey Mum, I'm finished with my schoolwork; so now shall we make muffins?" Ellie asked, her eyes glowing.

"Well done dear, you did it in a blink of an eye. That's astonishing.", she clapped her hands encouragingly. "Yes, of course we can start now. First, you must make sure your hands are clean, washed thoroughly with soap and warm water, and then wear your apron and your hat so as not to get hair stuck in the food." Meanwhile, her Mum was cleaning the surface with alcoholic spray since she was a germ-freak type of person.

"Next thing, we can start it by preparing all the stuff and ingredients needed. Oh, and bring yourself a paper and a pen to write each step as we do it and I explain it for you," added Mum.

"Wow! This is going to be a lot of fun. I can't wait to get started." Ellie was overjoyed about the muffin project and baking on her own. She hurried to her room to grab a pencil from the pot on her table, along with a spare notebook. She ran back cheerily in a few seconds.

"Perfect! Now this is your apron; put it on," ordered her mum as she handed the apron to Ellie.

"Can I wash my hands later?" asked Ellie lazily.

"Nope, first things first. Your hands can easily spread bacteria around the kitchen and onto food, so you must keep this in mind before you start cooking any food. Besides, it doesn't take much time. Don't be lazy."

"Okey Dokey," said Ellie, doing as she was told. A few moments later, they started preparing by first searching for the required baking tools in the kitchen cupboards to have everything at hand. They both got busy bringing the milk, eggs, flour, oil, butter, baking powder, sugar, spatula, utensils, two separate bowls, electronic whisk, chocolate powder, raisins, and whatever needed in the baking process. They had a medium-sized old oven which, luckily enough, worked just fine. Meanwhile, Mum turned on the oven to preheat while they mixed up all the ingredients. They added chocolate chips to half of them and raisins to the other half.

Ellie was truly loving every moment, especially when she frequently dipped her fingers into the liquid paste, examining the taste of it by licking her fingers.

"Ellie, please don't put your fingers back in the bowl if you licked it clean with your tongue. It's just disgusting and unhygienic too." Mum gave her a sharp look.

After they finished filling up all twelve empty minicups, Mum programmed the oven to bake them. Ellie was overwhelmed by the sweet, chocolaty smell of the baking muffins. Her stomach was rumbling and her mouth was watering, hoping they will be soon ready to eat.

Meanwhile, Ellie got busy writing the steps and adding every small detail in her notebook on its empty page, making sure she didn't miss out on any steps in order to be able to repeat it the same way next time. She even drew some pictures to make it clearer for herself. After approximately fifteen minutes, Ellie sneaked into the kitchen and peered through the oven glass. She couldn't believe her eyes watching the muffins beautifully rising high which looked similar to the ones she had seen earlier on the TV programme. "This is *so cool!*" She jumped up and down on her toes with hysterical cheerfulness.

When the muffins were evenly baked and ready to eat, Mum picked a white ceramic plate and placed two of them into it until they cooled down a bit. Ellie took out a bottle of milk and poured some milk for them in two big glasses. She added some chocolate powder to hers.

As they bit into their muffins, they both agreed that the taste was awesome, and they had done a great job.

The following day, Ellie asked her Mum again to come and help her with baking the muffins. This time she insisted on doing most of the task herself and instead wanted her Mum to help only with the tricky parts such as programming the oven's temperature and time and putting them on the oven tray. Her Mum agreed with her and they both were ready in the kitchen. So, Ellie brought her notebook along with her, opened the page which she had marked it with a bookmark, and followed every single instruction as mentioned in it through her own writings and illustrations.

Ellie had spread flour all over her face without even noticing, which her Mum sniggered at her and told her to wipe the flour off her face. She had made a real mess around her on the table and even on the floor tiles. Mum suggested she clean it afterwards and sweep the ground at the end, trying to be as patient as possible.

They finished it perfectly as planned and put the muffins in the oven to bake. While they were in the oven, Ellie was curiously fiddling about with the buttons on the oven and mistakenly touched a button, which changed the timer, increasing the time up to one hour instead of thirty minutes. The time passed and muffins had already cooked for about twenty-seven minutes and were nearly ready to be taken out. The telephone rang in the living room and her mum went to pick it up and thus left the kitchen. Since it wasn't a cordless telephone, she had to remain seated next to it.

Mum and Ellie had their mind at peace that the timer was set for thirty minutes and the oven would stop by the programmed time. So, Ellie comfortably came out of the kitchen too and went upstairs to her room to write in her notebook about her first experience baking on her own. She was so deeply lost in her writing that she had totally forgotten about the muffins.

Her mum was still busy chatting on the phone, twisting and playing with the cord as she was deep in talk, speaking and laughing at her friend, gossiping about her children, and complaining about their bad manners. It was one of her friends whom she had recently got acquainted with at the 'Knitting Association for Women'. She was a kind-hearted lady in her early fifties whom she loved to talk to now and then. That lady actually LOVED to talk and ramble on for hours non-stop, which caused them to lose the sense of time. After forty minutes, Mum's friend finally finished her speaking, and she hung up the phone. Mum then got out of her chair and stood up. She sniffed the air. Suddenly, she realized a weird smell coming from the kitchen. Something similar to the smell of smoke. As she took a second footstep towards there, she grew certain that it really was smoke coming from the oven, filling the kitchen with its bad odour of burnt cake. She froze with a stunned, puzzled expression on her face.

"Oh, no!" she gasped. "What in heaven's name has happened? What's gone wrong with the oven?" she said in shock. There they were. The muffins in the oven were burnt black, looking more like charcoals than anything close to muffins. Yet by some miracle, the oven had not caught fire. Without knowing the reason, Mum realized the oven's programme hadn't stopped the baking on time, which was peculiar. She was flustered and opened the windows before the smoke alarm went off. Then quickly pressed the button to turn off the oven. She put on her oven gloves and opened the door. She put her right arm to her face, covering her mouth and nose from the nasty smell of burnt cake. She took out the tray and put it in the sink under the running tap water. *What a mess!* She thought, looking very upset.

Disappointment poured through her, making her cheeks red. She marched out of the kitchen and stood at the bottom of the staircase. "Ellie! Where are you? Come down! Immediately, please!" her hands on her hips, waiting for her to come down.

"What's happened? I'm Coming", Ellie replied from her room, realizing her Mum's tone was serious. She went down the stairs.

Mum looked at her. "*What* have you done Ellie? Fiddled with the oven programme buttons, I guess. Am I right?" She paused, then added, "One thing's clear, and it's the change in the timing." Ellie followed her Mum to the kitchen and craned her neck for a better look. She was taken aback and stunned, too.

"Oh! Um… yeah, I was touching the buttons on the oven without actually realizing I changed the timer." Ellie chewed on her bottom lip and lost her self-confidence even more in doing things which turned out as failures. Ellie hit herself on the forehead with her palm and said in a frustrated tone, "why do I seem to be always making a mess of things?" She stared at the floor with a big frown.

"Okay, never mind. Mistakes happen all the time; even grown-ups make silly mistakes. We can do it again tomorrow at the same time we started today and this time *you* set the timer and I'll watch you do it correctly. By repeating, you will learn each step better and do it more comfortably than your first time, and feel more confident about your abilities," Mum comforted her.

Then she added with a kind look on her face, "You know, everything takes some time to master and anyone makes mistakes before becoming an expert in doing something. First attempts usually suck and never go well," her mum reassured Ellie with a gentle voice.

CHAPTER TWELVE

"Good morning, Ellie! How are you? And by the way, how did your muffin project come along?" Asked Charlotte enthusiastically when she met Ellie at the front gates of school. A lot of questions came up in her mind seeing her friend after the weekend.

"Hey Charlotte! I'm good – great, honestly," Ellie replied, happy to see Charlotte waiting for her outside the building. Ellie's eyes flickered with emotion and excitement as she told her friend the whole story.

That day after school, Ellie hurriedly headed home to take her baked muffins to Mrs Todd, in order for her to decide whether to accept her muffins for sale, based on the quality and taste. In the last couple of days, Ellie had finally succeeded in making wonderful, well-flavoured, and tasty blueberry and chocolate-chip muffins that were moist and tender in texture and very attractive on the outside which made you want to gobble them up all at once.

Nevertheless, she had a feeling of nervousness and joy

pass through her both at the same time. She was on her way to the Bakery with the tray of muffins in her hand covered with aluminium foil. Luckily, much to Ellie's surprise, Mrs Todd accepted selling her muffins at the very first second when she laid her eyes on them. "Wow Ellie! These look marvellous! They must be delicious too," Mrs Todd commented on them in surprise with her eyes glowing. Ellie was flattered and her shoulders visibly dropped with relief. She let out a sigh.

"You have done this all by *yourself*?" Mrs Todd asked her while she put a muffin in the flat of her hand, turning it this way and that examining it. She stuffed one whole muffin into her mouth, nearly choking herself, leaving no extra space to breathe. By her facial expressions, Ellie could tell Mrs Todd absolutely loved the taste of it. It seemed as if she had become disconnected from the world for a few seconds when she was busy chewing and savouring every bit in her mouth, commenting with frequent sounds admitting its delightfulness. Watching her actually pleased Ellie, and her mouth curved into a smile.

Mrs Todd told Ellie to make at least twenty of them every other day if she can or three days a week, preferably. And as for her wage, Mrs Todd explained to her she takes thirty percent of the money of the sold muffins and gives seventy percent of it to Ellie. This was perfect and just about enough for Ellie. She agreed and made the deal with Mrs Todd the same day.

◆ ◆ ◆

It was Wednesday, and Ellie's class had swimming in the morning. Mrs Green took children to the swimming pool in the other building for lessons. Ellie hated swimming and usually tried to find a way out. Usually, she persuaded her mum to call in sick and would stay home. But today she had no other way than to show up, since she had used all her absent days allowed.

As they entered the swimming pool building, pupils all put their belongings in the locker and quickly changed into their swimsuits. Children wore their swimming customes and put their goggles on to protect their eyes under the water and pulled their rubber swimming hats on their heads. Then, when ready, they all lined up, standing along the pool. But Ellie wasted time and hid in one of the changing cabins, hoping no one would see her and she'd escape the dreadful hour. She was a terrible swimmer and Jane usually made fun of her and told her she swims like a baby. Ellie was afraid of the water for the fear of drowning.

"Where's Ellie, Miss?" said Jane slyly. "I saw her in the changing room earlier, but now she's nowhere to be seen," she said sarcastically. She enjoyed making trouble for others, especially Ellie. From Jane's point of view, those who weren't rich like her were inferior.

"Oh, yeah? Well, that's strange. I'll check it out," said

Mrs Green. She went towards the changing room and called Ellie's name. "Ellie, are you here?" she said, her voice echoing.

When Ellie heard Mrs Green calling her name, she panicked and her heart was slamming against her chest. She knew she couldn't hide there. She had to make an excuse for remaining there and taking so long.

"Yes Miss, I'm here… sorry I took so long… I'll be out in a minute," she stammered, not knowing what to say.

"Oh, there you are. I became worried. What took you so long? You better join the others along the pool, quickly."

"I was having a problem with wearing my swim cap, sorry," Ellie pretended, trying to justify her delay. Ellie came out of the changing room, where she was hiding herself, and with an embarrassed look on her face, she went and stood beside her classmates, who were lined up beside the pool waiting for her. Jane giggled and made silly noises for her.

Mrs Green told them they had to swim up and down the length of the pool four times at the sound of her whistle. "Three, two, one." She then whistled for them to jump into the water.

Ellie made a huge splash as she jumped in and shouted a freaking noise, moving her hands and feet like a frog, feeling panicky and acting as if she was about to drown. Children laughed at her behaviour and pointed towards her. "Oi, you red fish! Can't you ever learn to swim properly without causing so much mess?" said Jane as she chuckled with her friends. Ellie's red hair had made them call her these unpleasant names. The sound of their laughter echoed loudly in the pool and seemed to go on forever. Unlike her, Jane was a professional swimmer and had even won medals at regional swimming contests. Ellie was nearly in tears and her cheeks became as red as a beetroot. She wished the ground could open up and swallow her and she could just disappear forever. Charlotte wasn't there to stand up for her, either.

After a few days, Ellie became disappointed when she learned about the fact that her muffins hadn't sold much. And it got worse when over the next week as Ellie was passing by Mrs Todd's Bakery shop, she noticed the shop was closed and the blinds were down. To Ellie, this was strange to see as it was the middle of the day when it's normally open. There was a notice stuck on to the shop window glass saying: 'Mrs Todd's Bakery is closed, and we'll let you know when it will open'. Ellie's heart sank at seeing the sign. "*Ppppffff!* Just my luck!" she rolled her eyes. Later on that day, as Ellie met Charlotte near their house, she told her about the Bakery sign and the shop being closed till God-knows-when. Charlotte said that she had heard the news that Mrs Todd had a bad accident. "I've heard that Mrs Todd was knocked down by a car in which a careless young driver was sitting behind the wheel. She's broken her feet and hit her head quite badly the day before when she was coming back from the supermarket and was crossing the road.

"The doctors said that they expect her to recover fully. For now, she's only able to stay awake for a few minutes at a time before losing consciousness again. Unfortunately, she'll be in hospital for a few weeks," explained Charlotte. That news was the last thing Ellie wanted to hear and, by understanding this, she stopped making muffins.

CHAPTER THIRTEEN

It was nine thirty in the morning on a Monday. Ellie's Mum was lying curled up in the armchair in front of the TV, when she heard a knock at the front door. She could see through the lace curtains; it was a red Royal Mail van parked in front of their house. It was the postman. He threw an envelope through their letterbox. The envelope landed on the floor with a thump. Then the postman walked back towards his van, revved the engine, and drove off.

Mum curiously got up from her seat in the living room and walked towards the envelope, which was sitting on the floor to pick it up. They rarely received many envelopes, as most of them they received were usually the electricity and gas bills or letters from Ellie's school addressed to the parents. She bent down and took the envelope, holding it between her fingers and read aloud the words which were written on the front cover. It was from an 'inheritance solicitor'. She sat down on a chair in the living room and gently opened the envelope flap and peered inside it, wondering what it was about.

She pulled out the letter and unfolded it. She had to put on her spectacles to read it well since it was written in a small font size. The inheritance solicitor had sent this letter in order to inform her that her Mum had made a will a year before her death in which she has mentioned that half the money she had would be passed on to her only daughter after her death. Mum's forehead crinkled in puzzlement as she read on. It mentioned that the amount of money which was going to be passed to them was 15,000 pounds! She couldn't believe what she had read.

She was so touched by it that tears welled up in her eyes as she finished reading the letter. She was overwhelmed by a mixture of emotions at the same time. Initially, the feeling of sadness for losing her Mum who she missed terribly, and secondly a feeling of relief for receiving this amount of money all at once, which was a massive financial help for her. It felt like a weight had been lifted from her shoulders. She also felt the strong mother-daughter bond revive in her heart and was sure that her mother was watching her from above and was there for her to help her, as always. She half smiled as she dried her eyes with a tissue cloth and looked above and whispered, "Thank you, Mum, for helping me. I really needed your help, like always. I love you and you are forever in my heart!"

Mum decided she would spend a part of it on a gift for Ellie's birthday, which was a few weeks away. She couldn't wait for that day to make her daughter happy.

◆ ◆ ◆

It was a Sunday morning in the middle of March, and spring was on its way. A few weeks had passed since, and the weather had grown gradually warmer and drier as winter turned to spring. It was eight in the morning and the sun was shining brightly in the sky. But with the window shutters down in Ellie's room, it was hard to tell that the sun had risen. Ellie's Mum came into her room and sat at the edge of Ellie's bed and gently shook her to wake her up. She opened the shutters to let in day light.

Ellie stood up and looked out of her window and was amazed to see the weather so wonderful. The sky was clear blue with no clouds to be seen. There were blossoms on the trees and the street looked more colourful and alive; as if life had come back to them again. She could see some children riding on their scooters, playing noisily and enjoying their free time. And Ellie was absolutely thrilled about going to the Hyde park at the centre of London, where a horse-riding show and a show jumping competition were being held. She had heard the competition would take all day. Ellie learned about this show a week before and had asked her Mum to take her and couldn't wait. Much to Ellie's surprise, her Mum had postponed her sewing work and agreed to take Ellie to watch the show jumping competition. Ellie had been chatting about it with Charlotte in school all week.

She wore her bright pink jumper, which her Mum had knitted for her recently, along with a pair of white jeans and brown sandals. She wore her hair high in a ponytail and looked adorable. They were both ready, standing at the front door, wearing their shoes to go out and enjoy their day. Her Mum wore her hair tied up in a bun and put on her bright yellow cardigan.

They got on the bus and sat beside the left window. When they arrived at the park, the smell of barbequed hotdogs on grills had filled the air as the smoke wafted everywhere. There were temporary eatery stalls and booths installed on the grounds in which they sold candy flosses, popcorns, ice creams and also fast foods. The atmosphere was lively, and people were all laughing and chattering while eating their snacks. "Mum, can I have an ice cream now, please?" Ellie pleaded pulling her Mum's hand toward the attractive colourful ice-cream van which was parked there and played a music to attract more people to buy from them, especially kids.

"Okay… Okay… then I'll have one too in a cone," Mum agreed as she reached into her tote bag and rummaged through for her wallet. She pulled out her wallet and counted her coins and gave it to Ellie to buy them ice creams. They both had their ice creams in their hands and walked cheerfully towards the horse-riding arena as they licked on their cold treat along the way before it melted in the warm, sunny spring weather.

Along their way, there was a place where the trucks, trailers, and cars, which belonged to the horse-riders, were parked. They could see ahead of them were the riding arenas, in which many people were already seated. The show jumping arena consisted of plenty of seats which encircled the main field where the competition actually took place. There were several obstacles at different heights planted on the surface of the course for the competition. The course was made of sand and was 4,000 square metres in size. Generally, at their arrival at the show, before the event starts, riders have the chance to first walk the course get a good look around the place, learn the course which they will have to jump and decide how many strides the horse needs to take between each jump and from which angle.

Ellie caught sight of the many horses standing there, all in different colours and of different breeds. Each belonged to their owners, who seemed to be wealthy by their appearances. Having a horse meant having a lot of money, especially if you trained them for competitions.

Ellie was dazzled to see the competition horses up-close. There was a boy amid the crowd who caught Ellie's glimpse. He seemed very confident and was in his expensive horse-riding outfit, wearing a white polo shirt, a black blazer, white breeches, shiny black riding boots, and had a helmet on his head. He obviously looked like a rich boy. He was standing there with his stunning brown horse at his side and was proudly glancing sideways at his horse and patting it on the head and cuddling it. The horse was a Hanoverian breed by the looks of it and its physical build, thought Ellie. They originate from Germany. Ellie had read about the best breeds for show-jumping and had some information about them.

The boy's horse looked pretty similar to the one Ellie had seen in her dream a few months back and reminded her of it. It had its mane plaited meticulously and his body was clipped perfectly and was shiny and well-brushed. It had two white socks at the front legs. His horse stood 17-hands tall, his body had a strong build, and he looked powerful and intelligent. The horse and the rider both seemed to know what they were going to do and seemed at ease with each other. They had built a strong rider and horse relationship, which was evident. The horse started trotting and cantering as they did the warmup. It seemed like those intelligent and well-trained horses competing in the Grand Prix. Ellie could clearly witness the close bond they had together. Ellie locked her gaze on how the boy brushed the mane with a comb and tacked up his horse. He put the saddle pad and saddle on it. Then he buckled the girth under the side flap of the saddle and pulled it just behind the front legs to the other side of the horse under the belly and also buckled the same way on the other side. He pulled it very tight so the saddle was really locked in place. He jumped on the back of his charming horse and sat on its saddle. He warmed up his horse in the separate arena from the one which was mainly for the competition. There were nearly fifteen riders in that arena, warming up their horses before the show began.

In her mind, Ellie pictured the horse to be for her. The feeling was becoming more intense as she imagined that she really owned the horse. She couldn't take her eyes off it and stared at it longingly. She wrapped her arms around herself as she travelled in her daydreams by trying to block out the sound of yelling and cheering from the people all around her to not disrupt her focus.

CHAPTER FOURTEEN

The show started, and Ellie and her mum were seated in the audience in the third row. There were nearly eighteen riders competing in the competition. As the first rider, who was an Asian girl, started jumping off the obstacles and didn't hit the first and second barriers, was 110 centimetres tall, people all cheered and clapped their hands, praising her. Her horse was a beautiful snow white, which shined bright under the sunshine, making it appear even more dazzling. She double-cleared the course successfully without knocking down any pole obstacles. She seemed to have trained a great deal on the days leading up to the show.

"She's by far the best young rider I've ever seen," confessed Ellie to her Mum as she stared at her performance dreamily, wishing she was in her place. After the Asian girl rider, that boy which Ellie saw earlier during his warmup, came onto the field.

The Asian girl was still in first place and Ellie heard from a person sitting next to her that the girl had entered competitions all across England and has won many certificates and medals so far by the age of eighteen. Ellie was observing her movements, trying to take in and learn from her as much as possible.

◆ ◆ ◆

It was 22nd of March and Ellie's birthday. Mum had decorated the living room with colourful balloons the night before while Ellie was sleeping. She had also baked a big chocolate cake and designed it with chocolate chips and cream as the frosting. She had invited Charlotte and a few of her classmates. She preferred to keep it a small party.

Ellie was sitting on the sofa surrounded by her friends singing her "Happy Birthday". Mum emerged from the kitchen, wearing a paper party hat, holding a cake, and started singing as she neared the coffee table in the living room, which was already full of snacks. "Happy birthday to you, happy birthday to you, happy birthday to Ellie, happy birthday to *YOU!*" She put the tray with cake on the table and clapped. Mum put ten candles on Ellie's cake, which meant she had turned ten and had grown a year older. She then lit each candle with the lighter in her hand.

"Okay, Ellie, now first make a wish and then blow them out," said her Mum as Ellie was excitedly looking at her presents settled in front of her.

Ellie squeezed her eyes shut as she started making a wish and pressed both hands together in the form of praying. *I want to become a horse-rider and compete in the national competitions* she wished in her head. And then she blew out the candles and clapped her hands.

Then her Mum told Ellie to close her eyes and Ellie did as she was told. "No peeking!" her mum said playfully as she went to her room and brought Ellie's gift with her and placed it on the table. It took her a few minutes to arrange the gifts on the table. "Okay, now open your eyes!" she announced.

Ellie removed her hands from her eyes and opened them slowly. Suddenly her eyes became wide open as she glanced ahead of her, laying her eyes on the presents, which were all placed neatly on the table next to one another. They were wrapped in stunning, shiny pink and silver wrapping paper. Ellie let out a gasp.

"Oh my God, Mum! Wow! I can't believe it, you've got me all these presents?!" Ellie's mouth fell open. She was absolutely delighted and surprised.

As she started opening them with the biggest present first, which was from her Mum. Ellie became gobsmacked as she unwrapped it. "Oh, wow! Real horse-riding gear? This is incredible!" she exclaimed in surprise and utter disbelief. Words couldn't express how impressed she was. Her mum had bought her a complete set of horse-riding equipment and gear. There were white breeches, a riding helmet, riding gloves, black riding boots, a white polo shirt, black jacket, and an equestrian body protector for young riders.

"Well, I thought I'd buy you the required equipment for your show-jumping school lessons in which I've registered your name. And it starts in two weeks' time, so you must be well prepared." Said her mum and smiled with pride as she handed her daughter the horse-riding school registration, along with her riding school identity card for the entrance.

"You must be kidding me! What? Is this some sort of joke you're playing at?" replied Ellie, totally shocked as she put both her hands to her mouth. She immediately stood up and hugged her mum as tightly as she could and kissed her on both cheeks and said, "You're the best Mum on the planet. Thank you *so* much for buying me all these presents and for the horse-riding class... I think I'm dreaming all this." She meant it with all her heart.

Ellie's friends were also surprised and watched in awe with mouths open at what she had got from her Mum. "Oh my god, look that's wicked!" one friend nudged the other.

"Well Ellie, I am glad to see you so happy. I wanted to make your dream come true," replied her Mum, beaming from ear to ear. Mum was obviously pleased with herself for making her daughter's dream come true and making Ellie ecstatically happy after a long time.

Ellie opened the other presents, which were from her friends. She picked up one that was wrapped in a sparkling gold paper and started from that one. She looked at the card on it, which said it was from Charlotte. She opened it and she had bought Ellie a 24-colour acrylic paint set which she knew Ellie loved. "Wow! I badly wanted this, Charlotte!" Ellie smiled cheerfully and hugged Charlotte tightly, feeling happy. The other friends had brought her pullover, skirt, books, backpack, shawl, and a board game.

Ellie thanked all her friends and was excited and pleased with all the lovely stuff they had brought her. After the presents they moved towards the dining table which was mounted with various crisps, juices, sweets and candies, fruit bits, and sandwiches. "Girls, help yourselves, please," announced Mum, in between all the sounds and voices. They all wore colourful party hats and enjoyed their time at Ellie's party.

◆ ◆ ◆

It was a Monday and was the first day of Ellie's horse-riding lesson at the young riders' school. She had to be there at five o'clock in the afternoon. They started at five and it finished at seven o'clock. The school was far from their house and took nearly forty minutes to go from home to there by bus. But Ellie didn't mind the distance and was already so happy about being able to go to a real horse-riding school. Her lessons were three days a week, which meant attending on Mondays, Wednesdays, and Fridays.

That day, after Ellie got back home from school, she had a quick meal and her Mum helped her get ready, take all the stuff she needed, and put some snacks in her backpack for her to eat on her way. With all the stuff she'd packed, Ellie had a big bag on her shoulders, which made her look little. Luckily, the bus station was only a few metres away, so it wasn't too difficult for her to get there. She could easily sit on the bus with complete peace of mind without changing other buses. Her Mum kissed her on both cheeks in the doorway and wished her luck on her first day and waved goodbye.

Ellie felt a mixture of happiness and nervousness growing deep inside her. Her bowels started making noises due to the stress she was feeling. She didn't know what to expect at her first lesson and whether their instructor was good and kind or was an impatient and cruel type of person. Whether the trainer was a man or a woman. She was afraid if she didn't fit in their group and if her talent and abilities would be less than other kids in the class. *What if there are only wealthy kids there, and they make fun of me and laugh at me? Maybe Jane was right; it's a sport made only for the rich, not poor people like me. What if I don't have the required skills and competence? Jane had told me it's not in my genes to become a horse-rider, no matter how hard I try.* Ellie suddenly felt so overwhelmed by all these negative thoughts, she became sure it was going to be a bad start for her.

An old lady was sitting beside her on the bus next to the window and noticed the panicked expression on Ellie's face. She turned her face to her right, facing Ellie and put her frail, wrinkled hand gently on Ellie's lap. She hesitated for a moment, then asked tentatively with a warm tone, "Darling, are you okay? May I ask you if there's anything that's bothering you? I feel you're a bit panicked, which is not good for a lovely girl at your age." She had a kind, sympathetic look in her eyes. She had bright blue eyes, wrinkled skin with white, greyish short hair.

"Hello, madam. Yes, I am good, thanks," Ellie lied, not wanting to talk to strangers. She didn't feel comfortable to talk about her feelings to someone she didn't know.

"Well, however, I would like to give you a piece of advice before getting off the bus at the next stop… something I usually tell my grandchildren, too," she said with a heart-warming smile. "Life is too short to worry about trivial things, so have fun and take things easy."

"Thanks for your advice." Ellie managed a smile.

Ellie eventually reached the bus stop where she had to get off. She stepped down the bus steps and took a deep breath and walked towards the horse-riding school. With the words of the old lady, her self-confidence boosted a little and gave her the courage to take a step into the building with courage. She entered the narrow hallway and walked straight to the registration office. She was asked to show her identity card to be led to her training group. Hopefully, she was there just in time and the lesson was about to start. This school and their coaches were very strict about their rules and didn't accept pupils after fifteen minutes of delay. So, Ellie knew she had to do her best and be there on time if she really wanted to succeed.

She lost all sense of nervousness, and instead, the excitement took over. When she entered the indoor training arena for young riders, she felt such joy that she couldn't believe this was for real. "Whoa!" she expressed in amazement under her breath, which could be heard by others, and the instructor gave a little smile to her.

"You must be, Ellie, I guess?" called out the trainer from across the arena, who was standing amid the pupils who had formed a circle. Mr Harrison was their trainer. He was a young man in his late thirties who had already won a few gold and silver medals in the regional and European show-jumping competitions, and thus, was a reputable trainer. He looked serious but seemed to have a kind, understanding soul.

Ellie's muscles suddenly tensed at hearing her name being called out in front of others as they all turned their heads to look at her. Her face burned from shyness, becoming bright pink. "Yes sir, it's me," she muttered, her sound hardly even heard.

"Come along then Ellie and join your friends in the circle." He gestured for her to join them.

The first hour of their lesson was mainly about theoretically making pupils aware about the safety aspects which should be implemented in this sport from the beginning to ensure the rider and the horse's welfare and safety. They were taught about the basics of tacking up the horse, how to saddle a horse, and also providing pupils with a background information on show-jumping.

During the second hour, it was a rein-lead lesson. This allowed them to focus on the basics of riding in a secure environment. In the indoor arena, there were nearly ten horses for the pupils to start with and first get confident and therefore learn how to communicate with the horses.

After that, they were taught how to climb on horses' backs, getting comfortable with their sitting position and then doing the next steps as the instructor told them. Ellie was so nervous that she failed in her first practical lesson. She made a few silly mistakes and nearly even wanted to fall down on her face from the horse if the coach didn't hold her in time. At that very moment, Ellie felt the colour drain from her face. Her acts made one of the wealthy and mean kids make fun of her. His sound was echoing in her head as if it was going on forever. Ellie's face burned from shame she felt and wished at that moment that the ground could open up and just swallow her in and not be seen again. She couldn't believe she was ruining her dream from the first lesson and hated herself for it. *How could I be so dumb?*

After the lesson finished, she hurriedly packed her stuff in her bag to go on the bus towards home. Her shoulders were slouched, her face had dropped, and there was obviously no sign of cheer or joy in her expression. *Great! I completely spoiled it since the first*, she muttered with despair.

When she got home, she felt exhausted, which was mostly mental tiredness she was experiencing. Not to mention that she already had a long day at school and was up since morning. Her Mum easily spotted the sadness on her face and asked her about her lesson. "So dear, tell me, how was your day?"

"I ruined it, Mum. Today was my worst day and I feel like a loser," replied Ellie in a sad tone as she lay on the couch stretching her legs in front of her. She closed her eyes to feel disconnected from the universe and forget about her day.

"Oh, that's just not true and you know that darling." Mum went to sit beside Ellie and give her a hug. "I think you're being a bit harsh on yourself, since it was only your first day at a new lesson. Give yourself some time to adapt to a totally new sport," Mum reassured her. Mum stood up and went to the kitchen. She returned in a few minutes with a mug in her hand. She handed Ellie the mug, which was filled with hot chocolate. "Drink some dear; it will make you feel better."

Next day at school during break time, when Ellie told Charlotte about her incident at the riding school, her friend comforted her and said its totally normal as it was only her first try on a horse and a new place. Even so, despite what Ellie's Mum and her friend told her, Ellie was not convinced and knew it was her incompetence which caused her to make a mess of things.

It was Wednesday morning and Ellie was already awake at eight o'clock replaying the pictures of her unsuccessful attempts at the horse-riding lesson and being laughed at by her rude class fellow, in her head over and over to a point where she was afraid to go to the riding school. Her Mum came to wake her up, and she noticed Ellie's already awake. They went down for breakfast. Ellie poured herself a bowl of Rice Krispies but was too nervous to eat. Her Mum made her some peanut butter toast. She only took one bite of it and left the rest on her plate, untouched.

It was at three fifteen that day when Ellie reached home and had to take off her school uniform and wear her horse-riding clothes for going to her dreaded second lesson. While on the bus, she was replaying the scenes in her head again until she arrived at the stop which she had to get off the bus. She was there a few minutes ahead of time. When she entered the arena, there were four pupils already present and one of them was Tom, the one who made fun of her during the previous lesson. Ellie felt a tightness in her chest when she saw him and hesitated for a moment as if it's better for her to leave there, but she decided against it.

"Hey guys, look who's come!" Tom nudged at the boy next to him, who was also a nasty kid just by the looks of him. "It's that LOSER girl who nearly fell off on her face the other day!" He laughed hysterically with his friends.

Ellie was mad at him for what he said. However, she tried to remain indifferent and keep her cool and pretend to not have heard him. While her hands were shaking badly and her breathing had become short and quick, Ellie busied herself reaching into her bag, pulling out her helmet and placing it on her head, trying her absolute best to avoid those jerks. She took a deep breath and exhaled heavily, trying to block out the sounds and concentrate on what she had to do and get ready for the lesson.

The instructor came in and started the lesson about tacking (putting on the outfit and equipment needed to ride a horse) and untacking horses, grooming and bridling them. When they started the practical lesson person by person, it was Ellie's turn who was standing as the fourth person, to go front and apply what the instructor had just told them to do. She had to tack up the white horse standing in front of her. The first step was to secure the horse with cross ties. Next, she had to groom it and brush the horse. Then she had to place the saddle pad up on the horse's neck and gently slide it back into place. And at last, she had to put on the bridle (the horse's headgear).

But unfortunately, due to Ellie's high level of stress she was feeling, she kept on making mistakes from the start, such as dropping the saddle, which made Tom and his friends snort. "She can't manage the simplest tasks, let alone doing show-jumping!" whispered Tom to Alex, the friend next to him and they both sniggered. Ellie heard their voices and her eyes welled up with tears and her bottom lip was shaking so much that she couldn't stop herself. She was on the verge of bursting into tears and she prayed she wouldn't cry in front of all and be such an embarrassment.

The coach noticed it and hissed at the boys. "*Sh*! Stop making fun of her or I'll have you out of here!" said Mr Harrison with a tense look in his eyes. Tom rolled his eyes and instantly became quiet. By his appearance, Ellie guessed he must be a year or two older than her. He was such a bully, just exactly the way Jane was at school.

After she gathered herself, she could do the grooming and brushing with success and she sighed in relief, feeling much better.

When she got home, she went straight to her room, shut the door behind her and hurled her riding gear in the dresser and locked them up. Then she sat at the foot of her bed, hugged her knees to her chest, buried her face, and started wailing. She was heartbroken to accept the fact that after all this time, when she finally reached her goal, she understands she didn't belong to the horse-riding field and wasn't made for it. Ellie became sure about her inability to become a horse-rider let alone doing show jumping. She felt convinced that perhaps she wasn't made for the sport and second guessed her choice. She began feeling a sense of hatred towards herself and believed that she's not capable.

CHAPTER FIFTEEN

As the days went by, Ellie's mood was changing remarkably, and her attitude and manner had become annoying at home and in school. The pessimistic point of view had taken over her and as she felt more negative and poorly about herself, the worse her days at the horse-riding lessons became and thus the worse her performance became. Ellie eventually had come up with the decision to give up on her dream and was convinced that it was an unachievable dream which she should just forget about.

During these days, Charlotte tried to talk to Ellie about how wrong she was to misjudge herself so early in the process and scolded her. She persuaded Ellie to give herself another chance to improve, but Ellie just resisted listening to any advice and felt so down and pathetic. Gradually, her miserableness also influenced her relationship with her best friend. Ellie had fed up her friend by making Charlotte put up with her volatile and impatient behaviour. Charlotte therefore tried to keep distance from Ellie to avoid having a row, which became frequent.

It wasn't until one Friday, after the horse-riding lesson, Mr Harrison came to Ellie and asked her to stay after the lesson. He told her he wanted to talk in private. He had noticed the dramatic change in Ellie's self-confidence and manners and the fact that she was becoming a different person who had no belief in herself anymore and was jittery and irritable most of the time. When all pupils left, Ellie was alone with her coach and there weren't any bullies there to make her uncomfortable.

"So, Ellie, tell me what's eating you from inside or what feelings are bothering you." said Mr Harrison in a gentle and kind manner. He was standing near the horses and was patting on a horse's head while talking to Ellie. "Is there anything which is causing an uneasy feeling in you?" He looked into Ellie's innocent, bright blue eyes, then paused for a few seconds. "I would like you to confide in me like you would your father."

"I don't have a father," Ellie replied rather quickly with a sorrowful expression, which made Mr Harrison's heart ache for her. His facial muscles tensed when he heard this piece of information.

"Oh, I'm truly sorry to hear this, Ellie. I didn't know about that." He looked shameful and regretted his words in case he had opened up a closed wound. He patted gently on Ellie's shoulder and said, "anyway, you can count on my help. I'm here as your coach to assist my pupils in any way I can."

For Ellie, it was such a sense of relief to know she

could talk to someone professional in this field and be her true self, revealing her weak spots without being judged for her flaws. Besides, her gut feeling told her she could rely on him for help. "Thank you very much. That's nice of you," Ellie whispered back and looked up at him. The sense of feeling an instant trust in him and a start toward a good bond with her instructor became evident in her eyes and they shined bright, sparkling under the light.

"Okay that's perfect, then you can start with whatever that is bothering or annoying you, either inside your head or out there." Mr Harrison also had a daughter himself who was twelve and somehow felt a fatherly relationship towards Ellie too, as if she were his daughter and he knew her for long.

"Um… well…" Ellie hesitated how and where to start. She really felt the urge to tell him about her insecurities and get rid of her bad feelings weighing heavily on her shoulders over the past weeks. She continued as she started twisting and playing with her strands of hair. "I've always dreamt of being a great horse-rider and becoming a famous showjumper, competing in competitions and achieving medals and making my Mum and Grandma proud of me since I was a little kid… but as I started the real stuff, I feel like I'm not built for being a horse-rider at all. I'm just making a mess of everything each lesson and can't even handle the simple stuff, let alone becoming a professional showjumper!" she rolled her eyes, made a big frown, and pressed her lips together in despair.

"Mmm, I quite understand what you're saying, Ellie." He smiled softly, which made the corners of his eyes crease. It was only when Mr Harrison put a reassuring hand on Ellie's arm that she became a little calmer. "Tell you what, honestly, you can do anything you wish and become anything you desire. No matter whether you've got the talent for it or not, if you've got the right genes for it in your body or not, and so on... it's only important to know you can achieve your most-favoured dreams if only you truly deeply believe in yourself. Put all your faith in you and take small steps and progress one day at a time; That's what really counts at the end of the day. Never under-estimate yourself or judge your abilities poorly only by having made a few mistakes in the past. Mistakes are supposed to be there as a part of success and it's not called failure, but just meant to be a part of the real progress. Actually, your real problem, Ellie, is that you've totally lost your self-confidence in the first place and panicked and chickened out too quickly without giving yourself another opportunity to strive for your dream and witness yourself flourish. You are just being too harsh on yourself at the moment and beating yourself up for nothing serious." Ellie felt touched by his words, which sounded true to her and nodded comprehendingly. A half smile formed on her lips.

"Okay Ellie, I should go home now. You take great care of yourself and no bad thoughts anymore, okay?"

"Thanks Mr Harrison, I will try my best."

"See you soon then, Ellie!"

"See you, bye."

The next evening, Ellie invited Charlotte over to her house for tea. After school, Ellie and Charlotte both strolled off and headed towards Ellie's home. Charlotte had got permission from her Mum the day before to stay at Ellie's until dinner that night. The girls were super excited to go upstairs to Ellie's room and have a gossip session together. When they arrived at Ellie's place, they rang the doorbell. Ellie's Mum opened the door and warmly let them in. "Hello, Charlotte, it's good to see you again. How're you doing?" Ellie's Mum greeted her. "Give me your coat and make yourself at home."

Mum had made some wonderful ginger biscuits which the spicy aroma was distributed everywhere in the house, wafted down the hall and hit them as they stepped inside, which made their stomachs growl. Mum disappeared into the kitchen and began preparing tea for them by filling the kettle with water. "You girls go sit in the living room and I'll join you in a few minutes," she suggested with a warm smile on her face. She had worn a green dress with red flowers printed on it and her ginger-coloured hair up in a bun.

After a few minutes, Mum came into the living room to join them. Along with the ginger biscuits, she brought a pink flower-printed porcelain teapot filled with cinnamon tea, which she had put on a golden tray. She placed the tray in the middle of the coffee table for girls to help themselves. Mum believed having cinnamon added into the tea is at least healthier and more beneficial for the kids than having the ordinary black tea. However, she didn't let Ellie have more than one tea per day and insists she drinks milk instead, which helps her bones grow stronger. Mum poured them each some tea in those gorgeous dainty floral teacups, which the pattern on it matched the teapot. Her utensils were, as always, spotlessly clean. Mum wrapped her hands around her mug of tea, as she usually preferred mugs over cups since the content in mugs didn't finish too soon, as with the cups you only get to have a few sips and the drink was finished. "Help yourself, Charlotte," she offered. "So, tell me, how's school going?" she asked Charlotte as she sipped some more of her tea.

"It's not bad; busy with homework and school stuff like other kids, but that's okay. School is good in total."

"That's good to hear." Mum smiled.

Charlotte was eating some of Mum's homemade biscuits. "Yummy, this is the best ginger biscuit I've ever had," she said with surprise in her tone.

"Aww, that's very nice of you to say so. I'm really flattered by your compliment, Charlotte dear."

They all had a great time sitting round the coffee table talking and telling jokes, which even made them cry tears of laughter until their tummy muscles hurt. After having their tea and biscuit, the girls went upstairs to Ellie's room. Ellie lay on her bed and propped her body up on her right elbow while Charlotte sat at the foot of her bed, facing her. "Let's play Monopoly!" suggested Ellie.

"I love that," agreed Charlotte.

Ellie bent down and reached her hand under her bed, searching for her Monopoly board game. This was one of their favourite games they enjoyed playing together. They also loved playing the Brick game, and even sometimes played it with Ellie's Mum, which made the game even more exciting.

◆ ◆ ◆

It was a windy day with a cold breeze stirring the leaves on the pavement. Ellie wore her brown boots, with her striped blue tights, her blue skirt, a pink jacket, along with a green woolly scarf around her neck and put on her glasses. She often felt cold, so she preferred to layer her clothes and keep her neck warm since the weather could get so unpredictable. She wrapped herself warm, otherwise she would catch a cold.

She was going to her horse-riding school that day to meet Mr Harrison and choose a horse for her trainings. She knew she had to choose the cheapest horse to pay for the fee. Mr Harrison had suggested before that Ellie can help with the horse-care stuff such as shaving and cleaning them and helping with the stable work, and that would be in exchange for the fee she would have had otherwise paid. Ellie had agreed at once when he offered her such an opportunity. After Mrs Todd's Bakery being closed down, Ellie had to think of other ways of making money. She understood well that she couldn't force her Mum to work harder or longer hours since she was feeling poorly in the recent weeks which had made her take painkillers and go to sleep earlier.

Mr Harrison was already standing at the entrance of the stable, busy raking the hay. He met Ellie and warmly greeted her and led her through the stable. There were only three horses remaining at the time, which weren't taken by others yet. Which meant that those horses were not professional enough and not good for joining races. Their prices were also the cheapest for leasing, which was suitable for Ellie. The professional strong breeds were already taken by the rich kids.

As Ellie followed him, she glimpsed a beautiful dark chestnut brown horse which had gorgeous dark eyes and a fascinating curly blonde highlighted mane. It had inherited the flaxen gene, which had given it a lovely blonde mane. The horse was just so stunning; it ostentatiously stood out amongst the others, which made Ellie stop there, unable to take her eyes off it. Ellie decided immediately. "I will take this one, Mr Harrison."

"Well, let me see. Aha, that one there! Well yeah, that one. Her name is 'Dolly'. She is good for training but not more than that because she is too old for doing races."

There remained only two other horses for leasing; one was jet black, and another was a horse with greyish patches on its body, and neither of them appealed to Ellie.

"Could I have a few minutes alone with Dolly and take her around the stable yard, please?" she asked him kindly.

"That's not a problem… I will bring her out and you can see her for yourself," he replied with a grin.

Ellie held Dolly's rein in her hands and stood there in the green yard with its spectacular scenery and stared into Dolly's innocent, huge, dark eyes. She stared in return. Dolly was even more breath-taking up close. She stroked and patted Dolly's head calmly and cuddled her. She felt so connected and attached to her the moment she set eyes on her, as if she had known her for a long time. It seemed as if Dolly was meant to be hers. She craned her neck towards Ellie and leaned her head on hers.

CHAPTER SIXTEEN

The regional show jumping competition was going to be held in one month's time. During the past weeks, Ellie's mentality and point of view had dramatically changed, and she had become a positive thinker and was super motivated. She trained as hard as she could to improve her skills whenever she had the time.

Ellie told Charlotte in the playground how super excited and stressed she was about the competition, and she was really looking forward to it. Ellie pulled Charlotte abruptly to one side "Oh, Charlotte I just hope I would win a medal... oh pray for me please... you don't know what it means to me."

"I will pray for you Ellie," she patted Ellie on the shoulders. "Don't overthink, trust yourself and be sure that you can make it! I believe in you Ellie."

"Thank you, Charlotte, I'm so grateful for having you!"

Ellie was keeping a record of her progress as the days passed by. She was the kind of girl who was enthusiastic to learn more and absorb all the different techniques the experienced riders used by watching the people she aspired to be like. She then applied those to develop herself into a better rider.

The whole of those days leading up to the race, Ellie spent trying to absorb everything she could from watching Mr Harrison. If she had spare time, she would listen to him teaching the other riders and try to take in as much information as possible. She used the information to put them into practice in her own riding.

But regrettably, much to Ellie's bad luck, as the days to the competition were becoming closer with only less than two weeks left, Dolly became badly injured. This incident had occurred just as Ellie was riding during one of her jumping sessions, practicing for the competition with Dolly in the yard, jumping over some obstacles and oxers. Due to the wrong pacing and making a mistake in the number of strides, Ellie and Dolly ended up jumping straight into the oxer. This consequently caused Dolly to become lame on her front feet and couldn't canter any longer and slowed down and took small strides instead. It was evident that the poor animal was in terrible pain. At that moment Ellie was totally flustered about what to do, and mostly she felt dreadful for Dolly and panicked. Ellie quickly ran to call Mr Harrison and let him know.

He called the vet and when the doctor arrived, he did a quick examination of Dolly's body and feet. He told them that Dolly should rest and Ellie shouldn't put pressure on her or take her for practice for a few weeks. "Actually, unfortunately she can't join any race and should relax to heal fast until she has a full recovery and gets back to her normal health status," the doctor informed Ellie, prescribed some painkillers for Dolly, and handed the paper to Ellie. Ellie sighed in defeat. She had to forget about the competition now and knew her dream was ending. That day, as Mr Harrison saw the problem, he felt pity for Ellie and thus suggested Ellie to take his horse for the race and start practicing with his and totally forget about the idea of taking Dolly for practices.

Mr Harrison's horse, which was given in the place of Dolly, was a black horse and his name was Thunder. Ellie thought the name suited it well as the horse was a little too stubborn and hyperactive and didn't seem to get along well with Ellie from the first moment she sat on his back. Thunder did sidekicks and strange jumps, showing his disapproval and protest. He was acting bizarre and didn't listen to Ellie's orders, and even it wanted to throw Ellie off his back. "You, stupid horse! You have a problem with me, don't you?" barked Ellie as she was laying splayed out on the grass and her clothes were stained with mud. Thunder flicked his ears and avoided looking at Ellie.

A few days later, Ellie had enough of practicing with Thunder and gave him back to Mr Harrison. "I'm done with him! I'd be surprised if I'd be alive with him."

"Oh, and why is that?" he asked with a frown on his face. He added thoughtfully, "I thought you two have got along perfectly with each other since Thunder is a great horse and you are a talented horse-rider as far as I know, but now I'm surprised to hear so." His disappointment clearly showed on his face and Ellie didn't want to disappoint him; he felt like a father to her. "But if you're saying so, I trust you and we'll have to see what we can do then. Don't worry."

Mr Harrison immediately made a phone call to the stable manager with his cell phone, asking for their remaining horses in their horse-riding school's stable. After he hung up the phone, he felt hopeless. He just learned that the two remaining horses were also rented recently, and he didn't have a clue what to do for Ellie, and he didn't want to let her down, either.

"Maybe we can hope and pray for Dolly's improvement in the meantime," he said, turning to Ellie and trying to sound hopeful – however, he wasn't.

"I hope she would have a fast recovery." Ellie squeezed her eyes shut and formed her hands in a praying gesture. However, she didn't believe Dolly would recover soon.

Ellie was very upset, and sat awake at nights just visualising about the competition which she no longer could join. During the days after school, Ellie would pay a visit to Dolly and check on her and see if she had improved. But no signs of improvement were to be seen. This dispirited Ellie so much. When Ellie was sad and upset, Dolly just looked at her and leant her head against Ellie's shoulders as if to apologise and sympathise with her. It was as if Dolly could read through Ellie's mind and knew how she was feeling so down during these days, which were getting closer to the competition, but was in pain and knew she couldn't be of any help to Ellie.

It wasn't until four days left to the competition when while Ellie was at her desk hardly managing to do her homework, Mr Harrison called Ellie's house. It was four o'clock and Ellie's Mum was at work in the boutique and thus Ellie was alone. She ran downstairs, holding her left hand on the handrails in her stripy pyjamas and her messy red hair flying in the air, while she dashed onto the first floor to pick up the phone.

"Hello?"

"Hello Ellie, it's me. How are you?" Ellie instantly noticed Mr Harrison's cheerful voice at the other end. She was happy to hear his voice and smiled. He felt like a father to Ellie and she called herself lucky to have such a caring father.

"Thank you! How are you Mr Harrison?" Ellie was gripping the phone hard with her both hands, pressing it as if the harder she pressed she could hope for some good news from him.

"I have a piece of good news to tell you, Ellie. Guess what?" he said with joy in his voice.

"Oh, really?" Ellie was fumbling with the phone cord, impatient to hear what news he had for her.

"You're a lucky girl, Ellie. Today an old friend of mine

who is a professional horse-rider rang me about half an hour ago to tell me he can lend his racehorse, Rosie, to you. He said you can take her for trainings and to the race!" Tony was his friend who had trained up Rosie from a young age.

"Wow! This is amazing. I can't believe it! He must be a very kind person. I really am a lucky girl after all!" replied Ellie, laughing with delight and grinning from ear to ear.

"Well, I guess you are," he giggled too and was relieved to be helping her. "You can come and see your new horse if you can today?" he suggested.

"Of course, I'd love to see her and can't wait for it."

When Ellie hung up, she sprang out of her seat and immediately put on her warm clothes to go out and see the horse. She picked a piece of notepaper from the phone table and wrote for her Mum to inform her about leaving home to go to the horse-riding school. She didn't want to call her Mum during her work hours and interrupt her.

At six o'clock Ellie arrived at the stable and spotted Mr Harrison cantering Rosie round the outdoor school. Ellie was feeling nervous to have a sit on her as soon as possible since a rider never knows what a horse is going to be like until they do. Ellie knew how crucial it was to have a horse that wants to work with its rider and how the partnership between them was important to perform well at a show.

When She met Rosie and stared into those huge dark

innocent eyes, it seemed obvious that Rosie could be a perfect horse for Ellie. Rosie was talented, sociable, and powerful with strong hind legs. She was a horse with great potential and had already won medals for her owner, Tony. Rosie looked like she'd be so much fun to ride. Ellie could suddenly feel how much she could achieve with Rosie. *It is as though everything that has happened, has happened for a reason.* Ellie was certain.

She was ready and motivated to start the practices with Rosie. Ellie understood well that if she wanted her dream to come true, she had to fight for it and let nothing stand in her way.

In the days leading to the competition, Ellie and Rosie spent as much time together as possible to train hard and jump over different heights. Rosie did her best to win Ellie a medal. Ellie was immensely touched by the responsibility and commitment which Rosie felt towards her.

CHAPTER SEVENTEEN

T he early morning light brightened up Ellie's room. She had forgotten to shut the blinds and had to put a hand in front of her eyes to diffuse the light piercing her eyes. Ellie jumped out of bed, awakened by the brightness. It was eight-thirty in the morning and at the same time, her alarm clock, which she had set the night before, went off. She hit the clock to shut up the sound. She went downstairs to the bathroom as she was feeling nervous to go to the loo.

It's the day of my show-jumping competition today! Ellie was standing in the bathroom washing her hands in the sink under the warm tap water and staring into the mirror. *Today I'm going to win! I will impress my Mum and Mr Harrison!* She smiled from ear to ear and her eyes were sparkling. She washed her face and combed her hair as best as possible and wore it up in a ponytail to look like professional horse-riders in the field, then she sprayed her Mum's perfume onto her neck and hair, feeling glorious. She skipped upstairs to change into her riding outfit. Ellie was so excited and full of energy and ambition that she could run the whole way to the competition arena on foot.

"Ellie?! You'll be late. Come down and have something to eat. You can't go on an empty stomach!" her Mum called from downstairs, feeling nervous.

"I'm coming in a minute, Mum!" Ellie shouted from her room as she was hurriedly putting on her clothes.

Charlotte's mum was supposed to come pick them up and take Ellie and her Mum to the place in which the competition was being held. Ellie was ready, and they both stood at the front door of their house. Moments later, they spotted Charlotte's mum's white car in the distance as it was nearing their house. In a few seconds, it arrived and screeched to a halt as the left tyre went onto the kerb. All four of them were sitting happily inside the car, chatting nonstop on their way to their destination. Ellie was feeling nervous but tried to shake off the feeling by engaging herself in the conversations.

"Ellie dear, how're you feeling?" Charlotte's mum turned around to look at Ellie face-to-face while they were waiting at a red light. "You look marvellous and I'm sure you're going to win a medal today!"

"I'm good thanks, nervous, but it's quite normal, I guess. And thank you for your compliment!" Ellie smiled, feeling much better than just seconds ago.

"Goodness gracious! This is ridiculous. I just don't understand why the traffic is so heavy today of all days! I pass this route every other day and I've never seen such a thing!" Charlotte's mum had begun panicking and was nervous she wouldn't get Ellie to the competition place in time. The cars seemed to not move an inch; they were already ten minutes behind schedule. This made Ellie sweat nervously, which caused round wet circles under the armpits of her polo shirt. She was squeezing her fingers and her toes in her boots to calm her nerves. She couldn't believe her bad luck. *What if I miss the competition just by being stuck in a crazy traffic jam?! No, this can't happen!* Ellie swallowed her saliva and licked her dry lips. She was chewing her bottom lips and couldn't help it.

Their car clutch was overheated, giving off a bad burning odour. It was becoming hard when Charlotte's mum pressed it. "Hey guys, I'm afraid if the clutch makes a problem, we'll need to get a taxi and let the clutch cool down."

"Oh, my gosh!! How can I always be doomed?" Ellie gasped and put her face in between her hands. The passengers in the car had kept quiet, just wishing and praying for some miracle to open the streets so they would drive fast, letting the clutch some time to cool down, and, of course, to get there on time.

They witnessed the police cars and ambulance emerge. They learned there had been an accident on the highway and that was the reason for the congestion and blocking of the highway. Four cars had crashed into one another and thus had created chaos. But as luck would have it, after a few excruciatingly long minutes, the cars suddenly started moving, and the police had opened the path on the right side of the highway, as the accident had occurred on the left side. They sped up and continued down the highway with the highest legal speed limit.

After being through a great deal of stress, they finally got close to the competition field. Charlotte's mum pushed her foot harder on the accelerator pedal to get to the car park as soon as possible since they only had five minutes left to the start of the programme.

"Phew! We finally got here. I don't believe it!" said Charlotte's mum and Ellie in unison. Ellie got ready to just jump down from the car when they got near the entrance. She jolted the car door open, climbed down from the car and ran towards the entrance while the others remained inside the car, looking for the first empty parking space.

"We'll be there in no time darling!" shouted her Mum from inside the car.

Ellie's forehead was covered in sweat and she was breathing short hard breaths as she spotted her team-mates, quickly joined them, and got prepared.

Ellie was a totally different girl than who she was. She had gained the self-confidence and high self-esteem she needed to have since the first lesson and had also developed the faith and trust which she never had in herself. Ellie had put on her perfectly white breeches, her black riding boots, her newly bought black blazer with a white polo shirt under it. She looked flawless and stunning, and her face glowed. Ellie gloriously entered the big outdoor training arena in which the riders warmed up before the competition began. The sun was shining brightly, high in the soft, clear, blue sky. Ellie and her teammates began their warm-up process with their horses. Some horses looked as though they weren't even tended to or cared for. There was a horse which looked muddy. Obviously, the rider hadn't taken care of the grooming and cleaning of the poor thing. On the other hand, Ellie's horse, Rosie, looked stunning and super clean among the crowd of other horses and riders with her meticulously plaited white mane, and shiny, well-groomed, strong-built white body. Rosie's huge black eyes were just so breath-taking when you stared at them, you couldn't take your eyes off them. She was the type of horse which would want you to cuddle her and stroke her all the time. She was sympathetic and made a great partnership with her owner. At the same she was just the right type of horse for showing all her talents in the arena and doing her best to please Ellie. She was an energetic, intelligent, and active young horse, which made any rider proud of having her.

The relationship and strong emotional bond between Ellie and Rosie were clear and they both could trust one another, even in the most stressful situations. They could easily communicate with each other and there was a deep level of understanding between the two. This is what any rider would ever wish for, and Ellie really thought herself as a lucky girl.

After the half an hour of warming up, the competitors had to enter the main arena. As Ellie entered the main competition arena, she spotted her Mum, Charlotte, and Charlotte's mum sitting on the chairs in the front row among the crowd who were cheering and applauding for the horse-riders. Ellie's Mum and Charlotte both had a big poster in their hands which were shot high in the air, written on it: 'Ellie is the winner!' and 'Ellie you can do it!'. Ellie felt so excited as she saw those big cardboards with her name on them. She waved at them cheerfully from where she stood and sent them kisses with her hands and blew it towards them. Then she spotted Mr Harrison standing close to the arena and waving at Ellie, wishing her luck. Ellie felt her heart thumping in her chest because of the excitement and nervousness she felt. For a moment she felt panicked, and her head felt light and dizzy. Ellie thought she was going to faint since it was her first ever real show jumping competition experience. It was local schools competing against each other. She knew that the time had come for her at last to show all the skills she had learnt and practised during the past few months. Today, in a few minutes' time, Ellie had to perform those skills in front of a big crowd of people who were all staring at her, being in the spotlight. Ellie told herself that everything would go smoothly, and tried to calm her jangling nerves.

The main competition field was quite big; a rectangular arena of eighty metres by sixty metres, providing sufficient space for the competition. It comprised twelve poles and fences as the obstacles for the horses to jump from. The height of the fences started from

1.2 metres. The horses had to jump a course of twelve obstacles. They should avoid 'jump faults', which is knocking down the rails when going over the them, that is worth four faults. Also, they must not make 'time faults' which means the rider has not completed the course in the time allowed by the course designer. For every second over the time allowed, one time-fault is allotted. And Ellie knew the rules perfectly well since she had gone through it many times with her instructor, Mr Harrison.

The atmosphere was intense and the thought of competing in front of a huge crowd of real people was daunting at first for Ellie. Suddenly she was having those negative bad feelings rushing in her veins, wanting to stop her proceeding and making her doubtful. *I won't let you bad feelings come inside my head anymore. You have no place in my head! And you cannot make me quit my dream! Get out of my head straight away!* Ellie whispered to herself as she tried hard not to get influenced and overwhelmed by her feelings.

Ellie had already learned the course in which she had to jump and the number of jumps they had to make together with Rosie. She kept the details in her mind to determine her paces beforehand, to jump successfully without knocking out any poles.

"Ellie Patterson!" Her name was called out over the loudspeaker as the fifth competitor, which echoed loudly and was clearly heard. Everyone in the audience cheered her as she went in the middle of the field sitting on Rosie's back. She felt her heart drumming hard against her chest. She put her right hand on her heart and took a deep breath. *I can do it! I'll prove Jane wrong, I'll show her! I'll make my Mum proud of me! And I want to make a great first impression on the audience today!*

Ellie heard the whistle blowing loudly, echoing in the field, which meant the race started. She knew she had no time to lose as the timer had started. She firmly pulled Rosie's rein, and they made a great start. As they successfully passed across the field and jumped over the poles in different directions at high speed, Ellie felt she was dreaming and this wasn't real. The time was passing by and so were they performing as they practiced before. She couldn't see or hear the audience. The only sound she could hear was the loud voice in her head telling her repeatedly that *she can make it, she can do it, and she can win it...*

There was only one more minute remaining before the finishing whistle blew and Ellie was focused on the path and poles which they still had ahead of them. They knocked down the last pole, which was the tallest standing nearly two metres high. Ellie's hands became wet with cold sweat but tried not to think of it until they finished the race.

After minutes of show jumping, surprisingly Ellie and Rosie had performed amazingly and jumped in the given time, knocking down only one pole. But still other riders were also doing great, and that meant Ellie couldn't be too hopeful.

At the end of the competition, when all the riders had competed, the commentator started announcing the names of the first, second, and third winners in the loudspeaker. "Ladies and gentlemen, now please be ready to find out who's the first winner! Who's going to win the gold medal today?" He paused for a few seconds to make the moment more exciting and breath-taking. "It's…. Sarah Watson!" Yelled the commentator in the loudspeaker. The crowd cheered her on as she went up the stairs of the tri-level podium to stand on the middle top platform when they called her name. Ellie had her fingers crossed and was sweating from stress. *What if I have failed? What if my name won't be amongst the three winners? Then I'll be a total loser!* She closed her eyes and prayed while her heart was pounding.

Then the next minute, the commentator called out the second-placed winner's name. "Okay, now again, I want you all to pay attention and listen. I'm calling out the second winner. Who do you think has won the silver medal?" At that moment Ellie could hear people calling other rider's names, hoping they had won, and she felt she was losing her hope completely as she watched the audience cheering and mentioning other names. "Okay, okay, so our silver-medal winner is… Ellie Patterson!" Her name was written in huge letters displayed on the billboard for the audience to see.

By hearing her name, Ellie suddenly let out a big sigh of relief and just couldn't believe what she'd heard. *Wow! Oh my God! Is it really me?* Ellie jumped high and punched the air with her fist and waved euphorically at her Mum. She yelled "Yeah! I won! I won."

Her Mum, Charlotte, Charlotte's mum, and Mr Harrison all came running towards her with cheery, smiling faces and eyes wide and sparkly with zeal, clapping hands for her.

"Ellie, you won! I'm so proud of you, my lovely daughter!"

"You did a great job, Ellie!"

"Bravo Ellie! You're a great horse-rider!"

Ellie could hear all these compliments and was overwhelmed by all those great words she was hearing. *Is this for real? Maybe I'm just daydreaming! Have I really won a medal?* The next second Ellie ran into her Mum's embrace and they hugged each other as tightly as possible for seconds and they both cried with happiness. Her Mum cried tears of utter joy and had to blow her nose in her handkerchief. They were all so proud of Ellie and she, too, was so proud of herself. As Ellie looked around at those who were clapping hands for her, she caught a glimpse of some of her school classmates sitting in the audience as well. Among them were two of Jane's friends. Ellie was amazed and pleasantly surprised to see them come here to watch her, and it really felt good to know they, too, were there to give her their support

That was the moment which Ellie had dreamed of all her life, and after facing all difficult times and barriers in the past, she'd finally pushed through and succeeded, which was all worth it. Ellie couldn't believe she had really done it and wiped her tears of joy with the back of her hand and smiled at the crowd.

The three winners had to stand in the middle of the field in the respective order to receive their medals. Sarah Watson craned her neck as she was being awarded her Gold medal by the former show-jumping champion. Ellie was positioned at the right-hand side platform, in the second-place position. And there was Tom, her rude and pompous teammate, standing at the third-place platform, having won a bronze medal. He didn't want to look at Ellie as he felt ashamed about being third. He couldn't believe Ellie, who he believed to be a dummy, had won a silver medal.

"Ellie Patterson," they announced into the microphone as Ellie bowed so the woman could drape the medal around her neck. All Ellie could hear at that moment was the sound of *click… click… click…* from the cameras in front of them, taking photos and capturing these cheerful moments to put in the local newspapers and on the school boards. They also awarded the winners' horses with a red flower crown, which they placed around the three horses' necks. Ellie was so over the moon fiddling with her medal on her neck and biting on it with her teeth as her Mum was taking memorable pictures of her daughter. Ellie wished her father was there among them to see his daughter and be proud of her. But she was sure he could still watch her from above and had become so impressed by her high performance and great achievement.

Ellie remembered her grandma saying, "When people die, it doesn't mean they are completely destroyed, but it means only their physical body is taken away from them, and they are still living among us with their souls, watching us, and even praying and wishing the best for us…"

After the photos were taken, Ellie stepped down from the platform and hastily went towards Rosie, feeling so proud of her. She stood at her side and put her arms around her lovely horse and planted a big kiss on her forehead. Ellie thanked Rosie from the bottom of her heart and was so grateful for all the amazing hard work she had done during the last days and the sacrifice she had made.

"Thank you so much Rosie, you're the best horse ever. You are so intelligent and strong! I really appreciate your efforts and if it weren't because of your talents, we wouldn't have made it!" Ellie looked at Rosie's compassionate face and kissed her once again. Rosie gave Ellie one of those long meaningful looks, which meant she was telling Ellie that if there wasn't Ellie's hard work, perseverance, and consistent practices, Rosie couldn't have won either.

Mr Harrison was just staring at them and took some beautiful photos, capturing the emotional moment. He wanted to post the pictures on his Horse-riding school's board. He too was proud of his student and was pleased with himself for not letting Ellie quit her dream, instead having helped her push through. This victory was so pleasant for him.

CHAPTER EIGHTEEN

It was Tuesday morning after the show jumping competition. Ellie was outside the school gates waiting for Charlotte to show up and go to the class together. She was wearing a lovely red coat which was her favourite colour, matching her bright orange-red hair, making it even more vibrant. She looked awesome and self-confident, turning heads. She watched a car screeching to a halt next to her. It was a metallic silver Mercedes Benz. The car was familiar to Ellie. She noticed it was Jane's mum's car. Yeah, she was right, and Jane's mum was sitting behind the steering wheel with Jane next to her in the passengers' seat. Her mum looked so glamorous and her clothes seem to cost a lot of money. Jane's mum had the same looks as Jane, as if she was her elder sister, with the same straight blonde hair and green eyes, but with the difference that she had cut her fringes. A few seconds later, Jane stepped out of the car in such an elegant way. Her shoes were always neat and polished. She ran her fingers through her long waist-length blonde hair and neatly tied it in a bun at the top of her head, waving goodbye to her mum as she stepped aside. Jane always looked charming, even in her school uniform. As she took steps towards the school, Jane found Ellie standing by the gates.

Ellie watched as Jane was walking towards her and didn't have a single clue what she was up to again. *Why is she coming towards me? What trouble is she going to make for me now?* Ellie turned her back and busied herself rummaging inside her school bag, pretending she was looking for her notebook or something.

"Hey Ellie," said Jane in a nice tone which surprised Ellie, though she still had her head down as if she hadn't heard Jane. "What you did yesterday at the competition was cool!"

This time Ellie raised her head and with a weak voice which was almost not heard, replied, "Hello Jane... Thank you!" Ellie felt brilliant and was flattered by her comment. She never expected Jane to say so.

"But how do you know about the competition?" quickly asked Ellie, feeling curious.

"Emily and Nikita were there, so it was them who told me about how you performed greatly." She gave a grin and strode off towards the school building.

Ellie felt very special and was utterly surprised to hear those words from Jane. As she entered the classroom and sat behind her desk as usual, suddenly most of her classmates came and gathered round her table. They all admired her and cheered her in the classroom. Many of them even asked her to become close friends with them and even pushed one another away to be the first to ask her. "Ellie, can we be best friends? I can teach you maths if you wish," offered Diana, who always did great in maths.

They started asking her questions about her championship and how she managed to do that. No one knew about her horse-riding classes except for Charlotte.

"How did you learn horse-riding Ellie?" asked Mila from the middle of the crowd.

"Ellie, I wish I could also be a hero like you!" shouted another among the pupils.

"I love horses too, but I never think I will be able to join a competition," said Mary, rolling her eyes with regret.

"How long have you trained for it?"

Ellie was too overwhelmed and surprised by her classmates' reactions. She was experiencing the most emotional and exciting moments in her life, so she was lost for words. It was beyond what she'd prepared for, and she felt she was the luckiest girl on the planet. Ellie had other friends who saw her skills and talents and truly believed in her potential. And they were all proud of Ellie.

The questions were going on nonstop until their teacher, Mrs Hamilton, entered the class. She had to make a loud, attention-grabbing noise for them to be quiet. She looked red, which meant she was furious. "What's all this noise? Go and take your seats this instant!" she shouted at the top of her lungs to be heard amidst the crowd of talking children.

That day Ellie went towards home on her bike as usual, but this time it was different. She was followed by her new friends, who wanted to be around her as much as possible. They made her laugh all the way home, telling silly jokes.

Since that day, Ellie came to school looking happy and comfortable. She even looked more beautiful to others' eyes. In art class, Ellie offered help to those who were not good at art and sat next to them giving tips since she was good at arts.

Ellie planned to go and see Dolly on Saturday after the race. She had asked about Dolly's health and healing process from Mr Harrison during the days which she hadn't seen her and was busy getting ready for the race. Ellie was relieved to know that Dolly had fully recovered and was perfectly looked after and in good hands.

Ellie had asked Mr Harrison to see Dolly, and he totally agreed with Ellie. As she entered the stable, Dolly instantly recognised Ellie and stared at her. She made a sound and flicked her ears in surprise and walked towards Ellie. Ellie ran into her and cuddled her as hard as she could, and stroked her neck and pressed her cheek against Dolly's. Ellie kissed her head and as she stared into Dolly's big brown eyes, she told her how grateful and blessed she was to have Dolly all those days where she had helped her to train and practice for the big race. It was her, Dolly, who gave Ellie the required strength and skills to win the race. Dolly leaned her head on Ellie's shoulder and was happy to see her again.

"I don't know what I could've done without you, Dolly. Thank you so much!" And as tears of joy were running down Ellie's cheeks, she kissed Dolly again on her forehead.

"Oh, by the way, I will come here again next week and re-start my trainings with you again," she giggled joyfully and noticed the delight and content in Dolly's eyes too.

CHAPTER NINETEEN

I t was Friday night, and Ellie was already tucked in her bed under her warm, cosy blanket. She had maths exam on Monday, which meant that she had to study hard for it to pass with an acceptable grade since it was their final exams. She had no idea how she could catch up with all those previously taught lessons, which she hadn't learnt at the time. Instead, she replaced the sense of despair with a big wide smile and held her smile as long as she felt good and promised herself she would do perfectly well as she had managed to overcome other difficult tasks in her life. And with that soothing thought, her eyes began to feel heavy, and she fell asleep.

It was the next day when the doorbell rang. Ellie was sitting in the hall so her Mum went to answer it. Mum opened the door. To Ellie's surprise, she could see that it was Diana, her classmate, standing behind the door. She didn't know why she had come for and remained seated in her chair.

"Hello, good morning," said Diana with a smile.

"Hello dear, good morning," replied Ellie's Mum looking a bit confused who she was.

"Well, I should introduce myself first. I am Diana, Ellie's classmate." She flushed a little, feeling she had interrupted them during their weekend together.

"Nice to meet you, Diana." Mum smiled.

"Actually, I came here to ask if Ellie would like to study with me for her final maths exam?"

"Oh, that's so kind and thoughtful of you, dear! Ellie will surely be amazed to hear this. Come inside dear and give me your coat. I'll hang it here for you."

On Saturday and Sunday, Ellie and Diana studied hard from early morning till late evening, practicing as much as they could. Diana taught Ellie a lot of information and on Monday morning Ellie felt ready for the exam.

◆ ◆ ◆

Three weeks later Ellie and her Mum went to her school to get all her exam grades. They met Mrs Bat, who was standing behind her desk, handing out pupils' results to their anxious-looking parents who had come along with their children to collect them. As Ellie was standing there alongside her Mum waiting for her turn in the long queue, she was feeling sick as she imagined the worst.

Finally, it was her turn. She managed to step close to the desk, where all the exam results were piled up neatly in brown envelopes. There were more than a hundred of them laying there waiting to be collected by the parents. As Ellie stretched her hand to receive hers, Mrs Bat shot her a not very pleasant look and handed out the envelope to her. Ellie shivered and walked away a little farther from the desk with her Mum and hastily ripped off the envelope and picked out the paper with the results printed on it.

Ellie had got a B- for her maths and a B for her science. "Mum! Mum, look at this! I've scored this high in maths and science! Wow!" Since Ellie usually got a C- or a C+ in these lessons, this already meant a lot of progress for her.

"Oh, darling, you really are an intelligent girl, Ellie!" Her Mum hugged her and kissed her on the cheeks, feeling proud of her daughter again. Ellie laughed happily in her Mum's embrace and when she spotted Diana in the crowd, they both walked towards her to thank her for the efforts she had put in, helping Ellie.

Ellie learned that if she would try hard to achieve what her heart desired and maintained a positive attitude throughout the process, she would surely succeed in the end. She also understood that failure doesn't exist, but is a part of the pathway to success; without which she wouldn't learn important lessons in life. And it's these hardships and trials in life which turn her into a stronger person. So she should pay attention to learn the lessons they give her, stay positive, try hard, and never give up on her dreams.

The End

Printed in Great Britain
by Amazon